DARK MEMORIES AND COLD BONES
VOLUME 1

Edited by Dorothy Davies

DARK MEMORIES AND COLD BONES
VOLUME 1

FICTION4ALL

TABLE OF CONTENTS

Iced
(Rie Sheridan Rose)

The dame walked into my life through the smoked glass door, all long legs and cascading copper curls. She slunk forward like a great cat on four-inch heels, a full-length fox coat thrown over one shoulder. Enough ice encircled her neck and dripped from her earlobes to fund a small country. There was money somewhere behind that three piece suit—not too far behind either. I wondered what had brought her to my dingy office.

"You're Sebastian Pool?" she asked, her voice warm honey with a whiskey burr.

"Yeah. Who's asking?" I swung around in my chair, hands clasped behind my head.

"My name is Clarissa Montaine. I would like to hire you."

"For what?"

Her sapphire eyes narrowed. "I need you to kill a man."

That caught my attention. "I'm a private dick, not a hit-man."

"I'll make it worth your while." She reached into her bag and pulled out a roll that would choke a horse.

My feet hit the floor with a thud. "You've got my attention."

"You ever hear of Simon Barstow?" She tossed the cash on my desk.

"The industrialist? That's who you want me to kill?"

"Would you do it?"

I picked up the wad and began to count it. There were more hundreds than twenties in the roll. I had reached two thousand bucks and not even made a dent. "Why do you want him dead?"

"He's my husband. Or, he was. He's filed for divorce and I can't have that."

"Why not? A pretty dame like you will find somebody else."

She dropped the coat to the ground, stalking away like a panther on those deadly heels. They clicked like nails driven into the hardwood floor. At the door, she spun to face me, chest heaving like an agitated ocean. "I don't want someone else," she hissed. "I want what is mine. If he divorces me, I lose everything. All the money, the prestige, the house. But if he dies before it's final, I'll get it all."

"Doesn't he have a kid or two from another marriage?"

"I can deal with them. Nigel wants to take his father's place—in every sense of the word—and the girls are easily swayed teenagers who just want to find rich husbands of their own."

She was cold as ice, this broad. I felt chilblains coming on just being in the same room with her.

"You've thought this out, I see."

"It's *all* I think about."

"Why did you come to my door? There are plenty of PIs in Chicago."

"I heard you didn't look too hard into where the money comes from."

"No, I can't say that I do. But I also don't usually go around icing innocent businessmen either."

"Innocent?" she growled, fumbling with the buttons of her blouse. "Would an 'innocent' man do this?" She ripped aside the silk and showed me several fist shaped

8

bruises on her creamy skin. "He is always very careful about the face, but anywhere else is fair game."

I frowned. This changed things. I didn't hold with killing no innocents, but I sure didn't believe in hitting a lady either. Seemed like the old man just might deserve anything he got.

"He hit anyone else?"

"I've seen him smack Nigel around a time or two. He's been smart enough to keep his hands off the girls, but I don't know how long that will last. There's a ticking time bomb in that house."

"So, don't you think you'd be better off out of there, even if you did lose the fortune?"

Her eyes blazed. "I've earned every penny of it and I'm not giving it up."

"Yeah, so you said. Okay, so suppose I decided to do this thing for you...where and when would you want it done?"

"You do have a gun, right?"

I pulled my .38 out of the desk drawer. "Will this do?"

A smile bloomed across her face, like the sun rising. "That'll do just fine."

***

She spent another hour going over her plan in detail. Over and over, *ad nauseum*. Guess she figured a guy like me was too stupid to get it the first time. But I tweaked to it right away. It wasn't as if it were terribly complicated. It was one of the oldest stories in the book. Girl wants boy, girl gets boy, girl wants to lose boy without losing all the benefits that came with boy. Girl hires hit-man. Bada-bing, bada-boom...

9

She would get Barstow down to a nightclub of my acquaintance in a seedy part of town. How she did that wasn't my concern.

I'd be waiting outside in the alley with my hat pulled low and the .38. He'd never know what hit him—and in that part of town, no one else was likely to raise an eyebrow over it. Wrong place, wrong time... gee, what a shame.

We set the time for that evening. No need to pussyfoot around now that the plan was in motion. So, I grabbed an early dinner at the Third Street Diner and was crouched behind a refuse bin in the alley by seven.

Clarissa had promised to have the old man there by nine. Better safe than sorry, I always say, so I was there early. Chain-smoking my thoughts into some sort of order. And what I kept coming back to was - what a horrible idea this was.

Sure, the woman had given me ten thousand dollars—which wasn't too shabby. I'd finally gotten around to counting it all when she left. But hating her husband was no good reason to kill him. The longer I squatted behind the spoiled vegetables and rotten meat the more convinced I was of that fact.

So, when at last I heard the sound of footsteps heading my way, I'd made up my mind about the situation. I knew something had to be done. If not, she'd never get off my back. It just might not be what she was expecting.

Clarissa wove into view, clinging to the arm of a handsome gent about fifteen to twenty years older than she was. It had to be Barstow.

She had left behind the three piece suit for clinging chiffon, but she still wore the fox, and... if anything... more ice than before.

10

He was trying to hold her upright but she staggered along. I was pretty sure most of her stumbling was an act. Even in the dim light provided by the single streetlight on the corner I could see that he was being most solicitous. He was also six inches shorter than her and looked so fragile that a strong wind would blow him away. Somehow, the beating story was losing more and more of its credibility the closer they got.

Just outside the mouth of the alley, they stopped and I saw the flare of a match illuminate her profile as he lit a cigarette for her.

"I don't know why you insisted on coming down here, Clarissa. It's a bad neighborhood even in daylight."

"You never want to have any fun," she answered and I could hear the pout I couldn't see. "Where's your sense of adventure?"

"I think I left it in my other suit," Barstow replied wryly.

I bit the inside of my lip to keep from chuckling. Good comeback for an old guy.

"Have you thought about what I said?" she asked, her voice sharp and hard.

"I can't beggar my family, Clarissa. I think the settlement I've offered you is more than adequate. After all, the divorce was your idea."

I drew my breath through my teeth with a hiss. So, the dame had lied to me.

I saw her glance toward the alleyway—no doubt wondering if I had overheard. Well might she wonder. This news changed everything for sure. My resolve solidified. Any feelings I might have had for Clarissa froze.

I hadn't been too keen on icing the man in the first place, but he seemed like an upstanding guy who wanted

11

to look out for his kids in the face of a greedy gold-digger. I pulled the .38 out of my pocket and steadied it across my opposite forearm.

If I didn't do something right here, right now, the bitch would only try again with some other poor sap. Barstow deserved better.

I put a bullet between her eyes.

She went down like a sack of bricks.

"You can come out of the shadows now," Barstow called softly, his voice steady as a judge. "I was expecting something of the sort when she persuaded me down here... but, I rather expected the bullet would be for me."

"It was supposed to be," I answered, keeping the gun trained—just in case. "She paid me good money to ice you tonight."

"What changed your mind?"

"Just answer me one question... did you ever hit her?"

"Hit her? God, no. I would never hit a lady."

"Didn't think so. Though she allowed that you did. Your son too, she said."

"Nigel? He's been at boarding school since before I met Clarissa."

"What about the girls?"

"What girls?" His voice was honestly puzzled.

"Don't you have two teenage daughters?"

"No. Nigel is an only child. He's fifteen."

She had made the whole thing up. Played my emotions like a fiddle. Damn it. I'd believed every word out of her lying mouth.

"I don't know what she told you, sir—or what she paid you—but you're welcome to keep it. I won't come looking for you. However, if I were you, I'd get the hell out of here before someone reports that gunshot."

I snorted. "In this neighborhood, I doubt anyone noticed. What will you tell the cops?"

"The truth. Some unknown assailant gunned down my wife before I could stop him."

I faded down the alley and took to my heels. Barstow seemed like a straight-up guy, but I wasn't pushing my luck.

***

It took three days for the story to appear in the papers. Socialite shot on the wrong side of the tracks. Police had no leads. Husband was devastated. Yada, yada, yada...

I apparently had gotten away clean. And I wasn't sorry for shooting her, either. Trying to hustle me like that... she deserved a bullet to the brainpan.

I went back to my daily routine, just a little bit wiser and a little bit richer. Of course, I didn't go out and buy a car or anything. I'd never be able to explain that kind of windfall. But it was good to know that I could pay my rent if the clients were scarce for a few months—like they usually were.

Three weeks passed like nothing had ever happened in that alley on the wrong side of the tracks. I began to think I'd gotten away scot free. I wasn't proud of what I'd done, but I sure didn't lose any sleep at night over it either.

Just yesterday, I picked up the paper. Above the fold on the society page was a three column photograph of a wedding reception. The headline read "Wealthy Widower Weds Again." The photograph showed a smiling Simon Barstow with a twenty-something dame on his arm cutting a wedding cake. The caption under the picture asked, "Is the third time the charm for Simon Barstow?"

I read the story in stunned silence. After the tragic death of his second wife, he had found comfort with his only son's nanny.

Yeah, nanny.

Nigel wasn't the twenty-something replacement for her husband Clarissa had made him out to be, or even the teenager off at boarding school his father had told me about. Nigel was four. Four! His mother had died of complications soon after his birth and Barstow had married her nurse—Clarissa.

Now, he was on his third wife in five years. Seemed nobody in that family was very good about telling the truth. And I was the patsy behind it all.

I wondered if Clarissa really did pick my name out of the phone book, or if I'd been suggested to her. Hell, Barstow might have circled my name in the Yellow Pages and left it out for her to find. I wouldn't put it past him. I think he had the brains in the family...

Neither one of them was worth a tinker's dam.

No matter what, Chicago might be a little warm for me right now. Time to bug out for a while.

I threw a few things into a bag. Most of the ten grand went into the bottom of the duffle. I'd buy new clothes wherever I happened to light. There wasn't really anything special in my apartment that I needed to carry with me, so I hefted the bag over my shoulder and locked the front door.

I was pretty sure I'd have no trouble getting away clean—after all, why would anyone tie Clarissa to me if they hadn't by now—and then I turned around and found myself surrounded by Chicago PD. I've always had a

pretty good working relationship with the boys in blue...
but their grim faces told me that my luck had just run out.

My mind raced, looking for a solution. Maybe I could
shoot my way out of it—but that would probably just get
me killed. I really wasn't interested in dying today.

Mike Murphy was a friend of mine on the force. I'd
been an unofficial informant for him and vice versa more
times than I cared to count. I caught Mike's eye now and
held it.

"I'm just going to set down my bag, Mike. No
trouble—okay?"

I reached for the strap of my duffle.

"Don't move!" Mike barked. "Stay where you are!"

I froze. His finger was much too close to the trigger.
"What's this all about?"

"I think you know very well, Pool. Keep your hands
where we can see them."

"Mike, you know me—" I just knew I could talk my
way out of this, if I could only get Mike to listen.

"Is this the man?" Mike called over his shoulder.

A figure stepped into view. "Yes, Officer. That is the
man who shot my wife."

Barstow looked bigger in the daylight—not the frail
old gentleman he'd seemed outside the alley. There was a
smirk on his face that I longed to wipe off with my fist.
So much for the "unknown assailant" story.

A PI is always just one step above the felons in the
eyes of the police. There seemed to be no doubt in
anyone's mind that I had done it—and I've never been as
good a liar as Barstow and Clarissa turned out to be. Of
course, the money in my bag didn't help the situation.
Especially when Barstow could provide serial numbers.
He played the grieving husband to the hilt, claiming that

15

his wife had given me money to be her bodyguard and I had iced her in return.

There wasn't much I could say against him. How could I refute his lies without telling the truth? Either way, my goose was cooked.

The trial is over. Guilty as charged, of course. Nothing left but carrying out the death sentence—they'll be doing that tomorrow.

But I thought I would write it down. I can't prove anything, mind you... but I have a strong suspicion things worked out just the way Barstow wanted them to. He got bored, or randy, or just mean and traded his wife in for another model.

Poor dumb Clarissa. She was as big a sap as I am. He used her to orchestrate her own murder.

All so he could sleep with another bimbo a little younger, a little prettier, a little... what? Guess it doesn't matter.

In the end, we both wind up iced.

16

The Danger of Approachment
(Dona Fox)

I dreamt I buried Robert beneath the yellow roses outside my bedroom window. When I woke, my body was sweat-drenched and someone had left muddy footprints on the inside stairs. I don't trust the new neighbors; with Robert away so often I must change the locks at once.

Robert's not to blame; he had to work a lot because he believed I needed material wealth to reassure me and though he'd never come home with a stranger's lipstick on his neck or the scratches of another's fingernails on his back, still–I sat alone most days and listened for him most nights–reluctant to be on my own. Yet I was certain I was a match for any criminal who prowled the night and I could best anyone that burst into my house. No, it wasn't like that. I was tough. It was myself I was frightened of.

I watched his car pull from the driveway, invisible bonds snapped, harnesses, safety lines–everything I relied on dissolved. My body twitched; my skin itched; alone, I became as naught, a void that ached to be filled.

Deep in my closet, I reached into the toe of the new Ferragamo's I would never wear and pulled out the burner phone purchased from the jumpy kid on the corner downtown. Then I opened last year's business directory.

There would be no record should the visit go awry. Again.

It's ironic that therapists never made me walk through a metal detector. And they never had cause to ask me for I.D. since my transactions were always in cash.

They didn't know me as I arrived in their offices broken. They only knew I couldn't fix myself. Oh, yes, they were all trained in the quick study. But I made fools of each of them and I fooled her.

I told the therapist I had an obsession with food, I lied so we could talk about my problem in the hope that she could save me. Help me to stop. Because I wanted to quit.

The doctor said my issue arose from a childhood fear of abandonment. Every one of them suggested that. I suppose they'd got it right as far as it goes.

I told her I always started small, one chocolate chip cookie or one spoonful out of a carton of ice cream, then I put the treat back—sealed up the package of cookies, closed the freezer, left the room. Suddenly, I'd wolfed down all the cookies, ate the entire carton of ice cream and found myself on the way to the store.

I didn't tell her my obsession wasn't for cookies. Or ice cream. Or for food at all.

At the end of my appointment, the therapist gave me shiny black capsules to curb my unbridled passion for food; despite how thin I already was. Oh, how I wanted to strangle her in her tasteless brown suit before she killed all her patients with her blind stupidity.

I have always been organized, restrained, but now, thanks to the capsules, I was also manic. I finished off 'so many cookies' I had no choice—because of spells brought on by the capsules, I planted half a dozen rose bushes in the backyard. Roses to hide my secrets. Perhaps I could at last eat enough to fill the void that gnawed at my insides.

Not long after I started taking the shiny black capsules, Robert quit coming home. A small splinter of doubt festered inside me. Had Robert returned during one of my organized frenzies—had I somehow not recognized him?

Because of my fevers, was he at this moment feeding my roses? Perhaps he was the shine on that perfect petal or the moon-twinkle on that gorgeous thorn?

I never talked to anyone on our street apart from the elderly Brewers, my previous next-door neighbors, I crossed the road to avoid every one of them. But the dear Brewers saw something needy in me and they refused to leave me alone.

Now I wish I'd stuck to that pattern, but darn, the new people who'd moved into the Brewers' house played their music loud enough to shake the knives off my kitchen wall. Jingle Bells. And it was August.

***

I hadn't meant to go into their house. It was the middle of the night; I was simply running over for a second to complain about the noise, so I hadn't changed out of my negligée. I'd slipped on the closest items at hand—my boudoir heels and short black satin robe with the ostrich feather trim.

The holly bushes at the bottom of their steps had tangled up my black satin robe. Its ostrich feathers seemed to quiver in fear—or, more likely, anger. The Brewers had always kept the holly bushes trimmed; prickly leaves had never caught my clothing on the Brewers' watch.

They were fastidious about their house and yard—and mine. They told me when it was time to mow my lawn or clip my hedge, when my windows were dirty and when they detected the slightest odor from my trash.

The Brewers never failed to save me from community embarrassment or the danger of approachment

19

by another neighbor. They knew I couldn't take care of myself.

Their departure was so abrupt–the way with people now, I suppose. Perhaps they were taken away by their children, illness, or sudden death. Even then, it seemed a quick goodbye was in order. Or were my thoughts jumbled? Surely I don't expect the dead to say goodbye to me. Unless they were quite close relations.

Anyway, because I was in a frustrated hurry and didn't want to rip the satin, I left my black robe draped in the holly bush, as if signifying a death in the house. I'd take the time to remove it as I left.

This new family, all the kids, the loud music. I wouldn't mind the music if they chose songs anywhere near my style, or at least in season, but they didn't and they weren't. The constant pounding from the basement– what were they building?

Or, wait, was it possible? Was the hammering, the clanking more ominous? No. I've been told that I'm blessed with an overactive fantasy life or a guilty imagination, as a former therapist had said.

Once in the neighbor's kitchen, I blew the curls off my forehead. "I live next door; the children let me in–"

A rotund man in Bermuda shorts sat at the kitchen table. He had a laptop open to his left and was furiously scribbling notes on a yellow tablet. His right pinkie finger was marked with blue ink. He made a definitive period at the end of a line of cursive then swiveled in his chair to face me.

He looked me up and down over rimless glasses. Suddenly I felt naked. "My robe caught on your holly bush," I said and to distract him from the hot blush I felt spreading across my chest. I pointed toward his porch, in case he couldn't locate his holly bushes on his own.

20

I crossed my forearms over my nipples while I juggled the icy brown bottle of beer and the warm doughnut the strange children had thrust on me after they'd pushed me inside and slammed the front door.

"Come here, sit down; what's wrong, Laura?" he said and patted one of his spindly legs.

I backed up. How did he know my name?

"Oh, I forgot how shy you are." His smile was yellow and crooked.

I was about to say, 'you don't know me; you know nothing about me,' when a herd of Great Danes came lumbering into the room. Fortunately, I pressed my back against the wall just before one of the beasts leaped at me.

The dog's huge front paws drifted down onto my shoulders. Oddly, it felt as if the monster weighed less than a pound. He was all tongue and drool and soon he had streaked my face with slobber.

"Down, Dasher!" Despite my distress, the man chuckled. His four chins jiggled. "Call me, Sam, Sam Clause," he said.

Good grief! He didn't think he was a beardless Santa Claus, did he? Meanwhile, the dogs were thorough in their investigation of my bare legs with their slimy snouts.

"Get your dogs away from me!" I stomped my foot. "Control your children." I handed him the beer. I'd keep the doughnut and, after careful examination, might even eat it, "and turn your dad-burn music down!"

"No need to use foul language," he put one finger beside his nose and winked. "I'm watching you, you know," he tipped his head toward my house. Looking at my home through his window, I realized I never closed any of my window shades, not ever–not on the living room windows, the bedroom and not the basement. I gasped.

He grabbed his stomach with both hands and threw back his bald head. He opened his mouth, revealing rotten teeth and as he laughed, a foul odor filled the room.

Once Sam had himself under control, he whistled and the dogs lumbered out of the kitchen. Somehow, one tricky canine had my doughnut in its mouth and my hand was full of drool.

I folded my arms across my chest, sped past the children and out the front door. I had to flap my arms to maintain a precarious balance in my boudoir heels as I raced down the steps, then I ripped my robe out of the holly bush, no longer concerned with the costly satin.

I'd go to the gun shop first thing tomorrow and buy the best earplugs in town. Only earplugs, nothing else–I swore to myself–though this was Texas and I could buy whatever I wanted. Whatever I needed.

***

I hadn't even crossed the front hallway when Sam pounded on the door and made me jump right out of my nightie.

"Hold your horses, don't knock my door down." I pulled on the remnants of my gorgeous robe and tied it tight around my waist, then I threw open the door. Sam's fist came flying right at my face. I jumped back just in time to avoid a broken nose.

"Take this!" He thrust a long bundle wrapped in baby blankets into my arms and knocked me over so that I was sitting on the floor with the package across my lap. He didn't even notice my fall. "Hide it under your sofa. Quick." He bounded off the porch and into the night.

Was I hiding this from the kids? Maybe it was a toy? A birthday gift? I shuddered–a Christmas present? So soon?

I peeked; no, it was a rifle, a real one. There was something sinful about a rifle if you had to hide it in the state of Texas.

Now my bottom hurt and my head was pounding. Were the cops chasing him? Were they coming to my door? Even more important, did I have any cold ones in my basement for them to find?

I tried to stand, dropped the weapon and cringed as I watched it fly to the floor in SloMo. Whew. No discharge. I picked it up and rotated it in my hands. No obvious harm to the rifle. I re-wrapped it, crawled over and pushed it under my couch.

My heart was stalling, begging for more gas when I heard howling coming from the backyard. The blood in my veins turned to barbed wire.

I leaped up and ran to the back porch.

The herd of Great Danes had jumped the fence. They were digging up my yard.

No. Oh, no. Not my roses! I threw off my heels and ran out, barefoot in my shredded robe. "No, go home!"

I pushed their muscled bodies toward the fence, but the dogs held their ground, sitting on my feet, leaning against me, drooling on my face and down my shredded robe, rendering the ostrich feathers eternally immobile.

***

The Great Danes would not leave my yard. They jumped the low fence with ease and dug with remarkable intensity. The enormous creatures had the energy to dig for days.

23

A spot near the rear of the yard, where my fence comes up against the back wall of the Great Western Savings, fascinated the dogs, but they were also interested in the yellow roses I'd planted down my side fence.

I put my hands on my hips and bellowed, "Sam! Come and get your dogs! Whistle for them!"

He didn't come. He didn't whistle.

I was fighting a solitary war in my backyard–me against his Great Danes. Pushing them away didn't work.

I got my shovel and every time the herd dug around my precious roses, I pitched the dirt back, fearful of what they might unearth.

The dogs needed to go home. Meat, that would do it. I ran inside, threw every bit of beef and chicken from my freezer into the microwave just long enough to get the blood running, then filled my arms with the dripping meat and ran back outside.

The dogs sniffed every bit of defrosted meat, then I threw it all over the fence, piece by piece, to entice them back to their own yard.

Sometimes I had to tear the treats from a growling jaw to throw it over the fence, but those shiny teeth were nothing compared to the thought of what the dog might unearth in my yard.

I did this until my freezer was bare.

Then I threw all the food from my fridge over the fence and the goods in my cupboards followed.

Sometimes a dog leaped over after the food and jumped right back, pale belly shining in the moonlight–it must have inhaled the food, though it could have been another dog returning. At first, I couldn't tell them apart.

In desperation, I filled the wheelbarrow with the dirt they dug from the deeper hole by the back fence and wheeled it over and piled the dirt around my roses. I covered my plants and let them dig the hole by the back fence to their heart's content.

I dumped out the wheelbarrow, again and again, until I'd buried all my roses beneath the dirt and made a massive bunker of earth over the rows of flowers—a necessary sacrifice.

Exhausted, I finally gave up and threw down the shovel. I fairly crawled inside my house; the dogs had won.

***

Bloody, sweaty, muddy—I collapsed onto the couch.

This time the tapping at my door was so light I wouldn't have heard it if I had gone upstairs to bed.

A tall, thin woman leaned against the door frame holding a cigarette between her fingers so she'd tapped on my door with her knuckles. The other hand was in the back pocket of her tight jeans. "Sam says your name's Laura. Mine's Marge. I need a quick favor."

It was well after midnight and besides, I really wasn't inclined to do a favor for the Clause's but Marge was desperate for her pain meds. She couldn't drive herself—couldn't see right at night—could only see out of one eye. And the meds were for her right knee, her driving knee. It might lock up again.

She hadn't realized she'd run out of the medicine until she went to take it and the bottle was empty—and being what it was, they'd only release it to the patient with proper I.D.

She looked down at me with big, round, damp saucer eyes. "I don't know what will happen if I don't take it on time. I'm hurting already."

Sam would stay and watch the children–unless I wanted to…

That was a big no.

I could drive their van–unless I would rather take my car? I couldn't remember what might be in my trunk. Heaven forbid I should get pulled over.

So, I was off driving Marge to the all-night pharmacy where meds were waiting for her. The inside of their van smelled of sour milk and the floor was littered with wads of orange and yellow fast-food wrappers.

"It's just down this street, four blocks," she said as she nodded with certainty. She sat with her back straight against the passenger seat. "no, wait," she tapped her window. "turn, turn here."

But it was too late. I had to go around the block. I got tangled in a one-way street and we were lost.

"The gas gauge is on empty." I looked at Marge. She was rubbing her knee.

"It doesn't work, but there must be gas or Sam would have said so." She looked at me with one eye; I didn't know if it was her good eye.

"So, where's this pharmacy? We're back on Main now."

"Stop!" she screeched.

I hit the brakes. "What?"

"Pull over, there's an ATM. I'll need two bills at the pharmacy." She pulled an ATM card out of her bra. "They only take cash." Marge patted my arm with thin, icy fingers, "right back." She tried to open the door then clicked her tongue, "only opens from the outside."

"I'll come 'round," I said.

Her door opened with the sound of metal grating on metal.

"I'm always scared here at night; glad you're with me." She dug her fingers into my arm.

"I'll watch to see if anyone's coming."

"Thank you, Laura."

She limped up to the ATM.

We were in the middle of nowhere. All alone. The sky was clear; I could see every star and had time to name them all. I was getting antsy. It was cold and I was barefoot, still wearing my tattered robe soaked with sweat, blood, mud, and drool from pushing, tempting and luring the Great Danes earlier that night as I moved dirt.

She clicked her tongue, "oh, no."

"What's wrong?"

"I forgot my code," Marge said.

"Relax, it'll come to you," I said.

"You don't understand." she came around to face me. Once again, she had tears in her eyes. "I was wrong three times. It ate the card." Her shoulders drooped and her body turned into a 'C'– "let's go home." She bit her hand to hold back a sob.

"I have mine," I said.

"I couldn't," she said but I heard the hope leap in her voice.

"Just a loan." I almost couldn't say it– "I know where you live."

I pulled the money out of my account.

Marge tucked the bills into her bra. I followed as she limped back to the car.

"Let's try again," I said. "Which way?"

Marge chewed her lower lip, then she looked at her watch. "Oh no, it's 2 a.m. Forget the meds, Sam needs me!"

***

27

When we returned home, the loudest alarms I'd ever heard were cracking the night apart. Sirens filled the air. Colored lights whipped up and down the street.

Sam jumped into the van, clutching a bag. He waved one arm up into the air. "take off, neighbor!" He didn't even have time to shut the van door. I didn't have time to step on the gas as requested before he screamed.

The van filled with red smoke. My eyes burned and I couldn't breathe.

Sam and I rolled out of the van; Marge, stuck inside, pounded on the window.

Sam was reddish-purple from head to toe, so was my lawn and the bag he'd thrown out on my grass. Sam staggered around to the passenger's side and opened the door. He caught Marge; they supported each other while they coughed and gagged.

In between coughs, Marge scolded him. "I thought you said they used GPS trackers now and even if it were a dye pack, it'd only go off if you went out the bank's front door. You idiot!

Sam spat on my lawn. "Guess they don't put all their secrets on the Internet. At least I knew not to stuff the money down the front of my pants!" He winced. "The packs get damned hot."

The police surrounded us and Marge hit him. "Wish you had," she said.

***

The room was small. I assumed the mirror was one-way glass. The detective said, "you were driving the getaway van."

I've watched enough television; I knew better than to talk, so I blinked and coughed.

Shouldn't he have another detective in here with him? Maybe someone else was watching through the glass, but perhaps we were all alone. His eyes were a tender brown flecked with gold, his eyelashes short but dark and thick. His black hair was buzz cut, but not too close. Below sharp cheekbones, his lips were full and tender. He must have realized I was assessing him. He blushed. I smiled.

Still deadpan, he went on, "someone dug the tunnel to the bank from your backyard."

My mouth dropped open. I dampened my lips with my tongue. I caught the detective watching.

He said, "if you didn't dig that tunnel, you must have noticed the digger or diggers."

If I said 'dogs,' would I be giving up my right to remain silent? I kept my lock on his eyes.

He cleared his throat. "The shovel found in the tunnel was yours."

I blinked. Of course it was.

"The rifle from prior robberies was under your couch. Your fingerprints were all over it," the detective said.

Under my couch. I was an idiot.

My wrists and ankles were somehow constrained; he continued to pile up circumstantial evidence against me. I found it hard to sit still, to remain silent. Should I ask for an attorney? No. I didn't need an attorney.

Though everything was true and incriminating, I was innocent. The whole thing was so absurd it was hard to keep a straight face. The detective and I should be sharing a cigarette, a drink and a laugh together. This was all too hilarious. An epic set-up. I wondered how the Clauses were laying it all off on me, if they were already walking away.

And to add insult to injury, they had my two hundred dollars.

I wanted to break my silence, but I knew better. I tried to send him the message with my eyes. Let's go have a beer. I can explain it all away. Just remove these restraints.

Please, look at me, can't you tell? Ignore the blood, I'll explain that. I'm innocent of everything, everything you've mentioned. Maybe I should talk. I sat up straighter and cleared my throat, opened my mouth to speak—

"No one at your husband's office has seen or heard from him for over a month," the detective said. "Do you know where he is? Can you account for his disappearance?"

"Disappearance?" At last, I spoke. The ill-advised word hovered in the air. I toyed with the idea, caressed it. Yes, of course, he disappeared. Poof.

"And why haven't you reported your neighbors' disappearance?"

"My neighbors?"

"The Brewers."

"Disappearance? The Brewers?" Now I was stunned— air sucked out of the room, punched in the gut—stunned. I'd liked the Brewers, hadn't I? I never messed with my neighbors; besides, they were old and so weak. And helpful. All their advice—their constant stream of instructive advice. I wouldn't have... would I?

"Here's why you didn't report their disappearance." He threw a photo down onto the table in front of me. I ignored the Brewers and ran my fingernail up and down the familiar zig-zag of the stairs I could walk in the dark in my sleep—undeniably my stairs.

30

"We found them tied up in your basement." His tone was flat.

"My basement?" A worm of fear birthed in my belly; I felt faint as he threw down more pictures and the horrid memories began to resurface. Sometimes I lost my temper. Afterwards I couldn't remember my fits.

None of this would have ever been discovered if the Clauses hadn't chosen to use me. Why had they destroyed my life? Was it the simple fact they needed access to my yard because it backed up to the bank?

I hit my forehead on the cold plastic laminate of the tabletop.

I gasped for breath as I felt the final tightening of the noose.

"Were the Brewers alive?"

It's Quiet beneath the Music
(Rickey Rivers Jr.)

I was drunk so I was stupid. That's how it went. I drank a lot, then I got stupid. Ordinarily I was pretty wise for my age. At least I've been told that before. I'm thirty five. Teachers used to like me. Friends did, too. People only hated me when I talked too much and got too drunk, or was it vice versa? Regardless, I never made enemies. But like the saying goes, one is enough, enemies that is. You can't have enough drinks. You can, but only when you can't drink anymore and you can only lie there in your own optional vomit.

And let me tell you, I've been there. I've woken up in other people's vomit at other people's places. I've woken up in bathrooms, bedrooms, backyards and any other kind of location you can name. I hate it, but I love it. I don't know what it is about drinking. There's love there, in drunkenness.

I've been tossed out of bars and invited back because of my company. I remember that, because I'd always go back. Bars can't stop a drinker. And bars keep popping up like liquor stores in poor neighborhoods. You'd think this country loved drinkers and drunks. The country supports us more than any other creed of person, be you homeless or disabled, you're not drunk enough for the country to care. Get drunker.

So with all this catering to us, why then are we punished for drunkenness? Don't get me wrong, I don't support drinking and driving or drinking and beating your wife and kids. I support responsible drinking. But it's impossible to be responsible all the time. There's always the possibility of getting carried away, before you're carried away, out of the bar, out of the party, out of the - etc. My story is about the etc.

I woke up out of stupor. Someone was banging on the bathroom door. I was asleep in there. That's probably out of order. After profanity from the guy who just pissed himself I stumbled back into the party. This was a friend's party. The friend's name was Stu. Stu's a party nut. We all have our addictions and Stu liked to throw parties, because that was the only way he'd get his hands on his two addictions: drugs and women. I imagine that's not the only way, but that's the only way his head told him it had to be.

"You can't get them otherwise. Throw a party. They'll come."

That way of thinking works for me too, let's roll with it. From the bathroom into the party there's music blasting and I remember being surprised the cops weren't called. Somebody usually called them at some point or other, but Stu was connected with somebody big, because the cops would show up, mention the complaint and leave right after. Then the music got blasted again. The cops never said anything about the smell in the air. I doubt they cared.

***

A while back one of the girls from the party came to my door. She was complaining and asking if Stu was alright. Stu owed her money. I didn't know he paid the girls to be there, but I guess that sounded like Stu, sleazy, loaded. But who am I to judge another addict? I told the girl I didn't know where he'd be at the moment. I told the girl I didn't care. Apparently she missed the last party. Either that or she was too drunk to remember what happened. She was distraught, but that's okay. It's Hollywood. She'll find another way to make money.

Come to think of it, I should have given her some money to stay with me. It being lonely at the top is a true thing. I'm at the top of this apartment building and every month I think about going up a floor and tossing myself off. The only reason I don't do it is because I don't want to be just another mediocre screenwriter who killed themselves because they can't get their scripts sold. Then the value goes up after death and suddenly it's "HOT NEW SCRIPT RECENTLY FOUND." And it's getting passed around like a hot new drug.

What a fate to live, to die, the in between is the only thing that matters. The party matters. Matters of the party went this way: a group of guys and gals were smoking and drinking and someone was murdered. That's the long and short of it. Somebody died. I don't think I need to tell you who the dead man was, or who the killer was, but I think you know. I think you know why Stu can't pay that girl her money.

***

I meet Stu years ago outside of a bar. He was arguing with some girl and the girl slapped him and walked away. Stu was consoled by another girl who was standing close by. Stu knew a lot of girls. He was a photographer. And you know what they say about photographers: know a lot, because they watch and wait for the perfect shot. You see, Stu took professional photos, but on the side he was something of a private eye. He got the shots and sent the pics back to scorned husbands and wives.

Stu was tied up in so much. That's probably why he was killed. People don't like you butting into their business. I honestly can't blame the killer. I know that sounds bad. Stu was a friend, but he was a jerk too and jerks usually get what's coming to them.

Look who's talking? I'm a jerk too. And I've got what's coming to me more than once. My face and nuts can attest to that. Don't make a woman mad. That's an impossible thing but take that advice. Don't make a woman mad.

Woman can be so vindictive sometimes. I can't even blame them. They feel powerless, just like men, but unlike men the world doesn't care when a woman speaks. Plenty of people don't even like women raising their voices. That's why I'm single. I can't take being with another woman, but I enjoy their company. I just don't like arguments.

I walked away from the man near the bathroom after waking up because I couldn't take his voice in my ear, his screeching. The music was different. The music drowned out all the noise of the people. People can be so annoying, constantly talking. Somebody's always complaining about something.

And I don't mean my criticisms of women to equal a hatred of women. I love women. Beyond sexual gratification I do generally enjoy being around women. I just get sick of them at the same time. I get sick of men, too. Everybody's annoying when you want to be left alone. People always want something.

I remember leaving the bathroom and watching the people dance around me. They were so happy in their drunken highness. I guess I was looking pretty happy too.

I danced with a few girls, had some laughs. It was all a good time, nothing but a good time. This is before the gunshot.

***

I got a call from Stu before the party was even thought of.

"Hey, Marty, how you been?"

"Fine, Stu."

And it was true. It was fine. I was living alone with no Stu in my life and everything's fine with no Stu in your life. Stu brings trouble. That's what the call was about.

"If I need you, can I count on you?"

I didn't know what that meant and I said so. Stu went on about getting into trouble with another man's wife, something about pictures. This is before I knew he was doing private eye work. But I don't think this had anything to do with that. Stu was upset. Then he was chill.

"It's cool, you don't have to help."

But he never told me what he needed help with. He just wanted to insure I could help if he needed it. Then he was gone from the phone. I was sitting there saying hello to a black phone screen. I felt like a fool.

***

I forgot to mention how I met Stu. You know about slap. You don't know about the fight. Stu saw me looking while he was being consoled by the second girl.

"What you looking at?" he said.

I still remember how stupid he sounded. I said nothing. I guess I was smirking because he said, "stop

36

smirking over there." Then he was approaching me. Stu and I got into a fight. I got the better of him because I know how to fight, with or without drinks in me and Stu didn't know that or anything else about me. After the fight Stu and I got drinks.

"You're a tough little monkey," he said.

And that was an insult so I punched in the arm and he laughed about it. I guess it was then that I started to like him. It's weird to find a friend in your thirties. Most folks say it's impossible, because people pretend to be friends in order to gain something or other. That's how it is with women sometimes. Sometimes you just want a decent conversation. You're not trying to take them home all the time, but assumptions lead to dumbness or something like that.

About liking Stu: I didn't like him in a sexual manner. We never got to that. I liked him like you like a friend. I think it's because all my friends were specters of the past and it felt nice to find a living friend in the present. Some people make you feel more alive. I felt dead thinking about the folks in the past. They weren't enemies, but you know what I mean.

Sometimes it's hard to describe the feelings you have for another person. Stu made me happy. It was nice to see a familiar face at a party, to see your friend smiling is a beautiful thing, to be reminded of the first time you put hands on each other, both of you looking stupid punching and wrestling on wet pavement.

The girl Stu was with was probably looking at us like we were crazy. In that moment we were. We were just two guys, who didn't know each other, who were soon to be friends, just rolling around fighting, bloodthirsty, drunken fools, drunken men seem to know friendship. We look for it at the bottom of bottles. We can't find it so we get angry. We start fighting. We slap and kick girlfriends.

The first time I saw Stu beat his girl was a terrible thing. Anger was hot in his face. I couldn't believe how hard he kicked her. Then he made it go away with a wad of money. Money is all you need to apologize. Money is all you need to do anything. It turns people into putty, pawns and prawns. Pawns or shrimp, take your pick, either one fits what I mean. People shrink themselves for a buck. What's integrity after all? It's only a word.

***

Another only a word is jealousy. It means something, but it hurts to talk about. I came to know jealousy over time. It felt like being ignored, bathing in embarrassment. I had no need for jealousy. It only led to heartbreak. If another person refuses your attention, you should always leave them alone. But it's hard to leave friends alone. It's hard to see a friend struggle. You're trying to help, but they don't want you around.

And why would I want to be around Stu? He was a terrible person. People knew. People talked. That's all they did. They always did gospel about Stu, his endeavors, his relationships. People love talking from outside the circle. When you're in a close knit circle things are supposed to be private. There's a lot you don't discuss outside of it. It's the same for family.

It always tickled me how people could talk bad about Stu and then turn around and attend one of his parties. They were two faced, but still wanted to indulge both sides of their neck. They loved to engage with the man they supposedly hated. Even the women who knew how he was, they always hung around. They didn't care. They knew drugs would be close.

And with drugs is money, they come hand in hand, hand over fist, if you know what I mean. And what I mean to say now is Stu owed people. Not only the woman that came to my door. He owed people promises he didn't keep. That's probably what the slap was about. I've been slapped before and deserved it. I didn't know who Stu was before the slap but he probably deserved it too. Whoever shot him must have felt the same.

That's right, the party, a bunch of music and druggies dancing. The music went on after the shot. Stu fell to the floor and somebody yelled.

"TURN ON THE LIGHTS!"

That's when we saw him lying there, clutching his stomach. A gut shot is supposed to be the most painful way to go.

"Shoot him in his fat gut."

Somebody said that. I overheard that, or I wrote that. I can't remember which. I drink too much. That's how it goes. I get drunk. I get stupid. I can't remember who paid me, but somebody paid me.

***

I had a screenplay idea about a guy and another guy who got together. They were supposed to run off with some money, or run off with some drugs. Either way that wasn't the point of the story. The point of the story was the fact that two men could find themselves wrapped in each other's arms and they didn't know what led them down such a crazy road. Someday I'll have to finish writing that. Someday I'll pull myself together.

It's only fun to reminisce every so often, but it's hard to do when you're looking at a bottle and seeing someone you used to love on the other side of a barrel. On the floor he had one eye to the carpet and the other eye to the ceiling and he was clutching his gut and all the druggies were gathered around and someone was guilty. I wish it didn't have to be him.

Is Love a Funny Thing?
(Rickey Rivers Jr.)

On more than one occasion I've thought about giving Donnie the old Farrah Fawcett treatment. I used to watch her back in the day, normally it was Charlie's Angels, but every so often you'd catch a movie she was in. I like the movies. I especially like seeing women like Farrah Fawcett on screen.

I think she was an underrated actress, in the sense that people only saw her as sex symbol, but as she got older they took her more seriously, or maybe it was her taking more serious roles instead? I think people only take women seriously once they gain wrinkles. You're only worth something once you begin shedding whatever beauty you were blessed with.

Did you know that Farrah Fawcett never won any major acting awards? She was nominated a lot, but she never took anything home. It's sad. She deserved the nominations and the awards. The only ones she didn't deserve were the two Razzie nominations. I don't like the Razzies, the concept seems disrespectful to the art of acting. Acting is something to be taken seriously. I always say that. Even comedic actors take acting seriously.

I tell Donnie all the time about wanting to be in those big movies, to be with the big name actors, getting awards for well-deserved performances, but Donnie says the same thing:

"Keep dreaming."

And I do and I have. I always dream. I've been dreaming since I was little, but I never dreamed of being on sets shooting people having sex. That's a dream for

41

people like Donnie. He's a director, but never the type for good movies, only the type for those movies.

Don't get me wrong, I like sex too. But there's more to life. I want more out of it. Sex is boring if you see it so often and trust me I see it a lot. I help Donnie on the shoots, it's a decent job with decent pay, but who cares about that when you're not doing what you love and what I love is acting.

I used to do some back in school. I was in theater. I didn't take it as seriously as I should have. After school I did some independent films and it helped me fall in love with the art of movie making.

It's fun to be on set, talking with makeup girls, checking out the costumes, watching over the beautiful backdrops and sceneries, script reading, getting into character. You got that stuff in adult films too, but it's different. At first it was hard to be in a room with random naked people, but you got used to the bouncing parts once you got to know the people attached to them.

There are nice folks in adult films. It's true, but people don't believe it. I go to the conventions with Donnie and we sell posters, DVDs and dolls with the actors around. Of course the actresses get more folks at their booths and some people even take pictures with me. Donnie didn't like it at first. Then he started charging people to take pictures.

I don't mind it really. I just don't like when the guys grab too tight. I don't say anything to Donnie, though. He's kind of off. He'd kill somebody in front of me if he had too, even if he didn't have to. Most girls probably would like that kind of protection, it makes sense considering the industry, but it's scary to be around somebody who would kill for you because sometimes you think "what if I made them too mad?" and "What would they do?"

And Donnie does get mad a lot, but he just throws stuff around the set. He never hit anybody he needed to work with. It'd be kind of weird trying to fight anyone on set with a bunch of erections around. At the same time, it would be kind of funny.

Funny stuff happens on set all the time. Adult films aren't all moaning and roleplay. Sometimes people fall. Sometimes it's like a hospital: optional piss, vomit and diarrhea. Sometimes the guys can't get up then the pills come out. Never did like pills, but they make sense for some stuff.

***

Today was a three way scene shoot, one girl, two guys. These scenes can be funny sometimes because sometimes the guys get too close and they get mad. But sometimes the guys get close and they don't mind. Those are best kinds of scenes because the chemistry between all three actors makes the scene come off well. Relaxing meshes with the goal of the scene. You want to reach multiple demographics. Women don't only watch adult films featuring women and men watch all kinds of stuff too.

All of us are unique, but the same in different ways. I've learned that over time. Women are no less perverted than men. We don't live in the old times anymore.

***

The job is also dangerous. People get hurt all the time. This one guy fell off the bed and it wasn't pretty. He

43

landed on himself, had to take a long time off, couldn't pee right after the fall. Another girl hit her head on a dresser and needed to be patched up. She kept saying she wanted to go to hospital, but Donnie wouldn't let her go. Donnie said the hospital don't treat sex workers right. At first that didn't make sense, but I guess it does. That's why you have to lie sometimes.

I don't like lying, but it's necessary to living. The world lies to you every day. The world tells you so much: you can be anything, do anything, go anywhere, but the truth is the world will allow you to only do so much. Anything more than allowed and the world will turn around and spit in your face. The world is cruel. Anyway, the girl seemed okay after aspirin and an ice pack. She came back the next day to finish her scene.

***

Sometimes Donnie takes the industry too seriously. I kind of understand because sex is serious business, but I don't like when he yells at people. People in adult films aren't objects. They're people too. I'm people. Any person in an adult film could easily start doing independent work or even go to Hollywood.

It's true. People always complain about adult film acting, but I've seen some terrible acting in Hollywood too. And adult film acting's not that bad because the women moaning really have a lot of erections believing it's real. The ego boost of adult films advance the whole industry and it takes good actors to sell a good product, direction too.

I'd like to see Hollywood actors jump to our industry and see how well they'd do under those hot lights with real penetration and a bunch of strangers staring at them.

Then again, who am I kidding? Some would probably love that.

There are a lot of pretty folks in Hollywood and some probably did adult films back in the day, their agents just had the tapes destroyed and anybody who knew anything killed. Some folks don't believe people in Hollywood can kill folks, but they're some of the most powerful people in the world because the entertainment industry runs deep and it's dirty.

Adult films are the entertainment industry too, but people look down on us and it's funny because we're the least likely industry in the circle to actually have someone killed. The music industry is absolutely poisonous. There's so much subliminal messaging passed around from song to song, video to video. It's kind of like our industry is when a new fetish is flipped and passed around so many times it barely gets you going.

Interracial porn, incest porn and whatever else is fetishized and made to seem appealing, but it's not. It's disgusting to sleep with your family. It's disgusting to want sex with somebody based off race and stereotypes yet we appeal to that. Just like commercials do and songs that praise sleeping around, doing drugs and shooting people.

The entire industry of entertainment is trash, but some bulbs shine through the dark and become something more, something greater than the industry their apart of. See: Marilyn Monroe, Dolly Parton and Farrah Fawcett.

**

I'm not a self-hating adult film participant. I don't even see myself as a participant. I don't want to be here. I'm here for Donnie. I love Donnie. Donnie takes care of me. My job is just a job. I like the people who work with Donnie. I just don't like what the industry's selling.

Donnie has to appeal to tastes, to fetishes. So shooting scenes with mother-daughter stuff doesn't make me happy, but I know it's not what Donnie wants. He's doing it because it sells. Anything goes when it comes to the job. We're selling a product and a product doesn't care about feelings.

***

One of the actresses spoke to me today and asked if I knew about Donnie taking another actress into the bathroom and getting a blowjob. Of course I knew. I just told her I didn't. To keep up appearances I told her thanks and gave her a hug.

She didn't do anything wrong by telling me. It's good to have trustworthy people around because the real world doesn't want anything to do with helping folks, especially in this industry. I decided not to say anything to Donnie about it. It was like an open secret anyway and what's the use in opening something already wide? That's an industry joke.

***

Donnie liking other women isn't new. It's a red bloodied male thing and red bloodied males don't care about nothing but satisfying themselves. I'm not fussy, so I don't say much about him looking at other women or grabbing, caressing, whatever. I know who he sees at night. I know who he sleeps with.

Some of the actors look at me funny sometimes when Donnie oils up a woman or corners one with 'words of encouragement' but I don't have a reason for jealousy. I know how men are and I know Donnie's only doing what Donnie does until he's done with this whole adult film thing.

You see, Donnie said one day when he's made his money from this job he's gonna cross over and start doing independent film, real serious, artistic stuff. That's the day I'm waiting on, my big break. Why would I let a little thing like sleeping around scare me off? Life's too short to believe in fidelity.

***

There was a lesbian scene today. I find it funny when people pretend to be different sexualities. I know it's for the money, but it makes me feel weird. Then I think about it being like acting in movie. You're just pretending, like being a superhero or a serial killer or the housewife Farrah Fawcett often played. She really was too good for the roles she was given. I wish she got rewarded with actual gold.

Women always play docile housewife type roles. That's why it was great to see Farrah break the mold and play different types of women. Being typecast is terrible. Even in this industry women get typecast all the time: you come in, play the teen, eventually you're the mature older woman. There's nothing to look forward to but being somebody's mother.

And isn't that just the thing in life? Women born just to bear children, it's a sick world. You have choices, but at the same time it's like your choices are limited. If you don't want kids people think there's something's wrong with you. If you're single there's something wrong with you. If you married too young you're a problem too.

People always complain about whatever other people are doing with their lives and their bodies. Why can't people leave people alone?

***

Today Donnie did a stupid thing. I can't blame him much, he was mad. I took the girl to the bathroom and cleaned up her face. Her lip was busted. I told her Donnie didn't mean any harm. She looked at me with teary eyes like she wanted me to say something else. I didn't.

It's weird looking at a person's daughter like that. She seemed so young, fresh out of school, playing a senior who slept with her professor. She shouldn't be here. She knew that. She didn't care.

***

Before Donnie went out I convinced him to pay the girl he hit double. It wasn't fair to her and I told him that. He agreed after some push back and said he was sorry. I told him I didn't need the apology. I guess men sometimes apologize to make themselves feel better. That's how it felt to me. Donnie is dumb sometimes, but I never saw him hit a woman before. I didn't like it either.

***

Today we had a roleplay scene with a delivery man who delivered to the wrong house. The wife calls the company and after some apologizing the man and woman get it on. Hollow story, but that's the industry. Shame is it could be much more. If only people tried.

I watch Japanese stuff in my spare time, not much of it is subtitled but they actually have a plot going on, acting's not bad either. Real interesting stuff, actual effort is a great thing. Actual effort turns me on.

**

I asked Donnie if I could do a scenario for the next shoot. He said sure. I did a quick write up and threw it away. Another idea came to me, one that I came to regret.

Today we did my scenario: a director sleeps with an actress. The director takes the actress backstage after accidently hitting her in the face. He consoles her with his penis. The title of the scene was: Somebody Broke Her Rear.

This is in reference to a bad review of a Farrah Fawcett movie, but nobody knew or cared about that. Regardless, Donnie wasn't happy once he saw the crew laughing. I thought I made it subtle enough, but maybe I didn't want to.

Anyway, we filmed everything and Donnie changed a bit here and there so my vision for the scene was completely lost, but it didn't matter much. The crew and Donnie knew the actual truth.

**

Donnie was upset tonight. Before he left he said some things to me and I reminded him about leaving the industry and making real movies. He laughed in my face. He said I could never make real movies because I didn't have the looks. I didn't say anything. I just told him to leave. Donnie's dumb, always been dumb.

I was told from another actress that Donnie's been seen around town with some other girl. I didn't say much, all I said was thank you. I think people know by now that not much bothers me. When it comes to Donnie I know the deal.

***

Throughout our relationship Donnie's never hit me before. I've watched him beat up a drunk outside a bar, saw him fight his way through a dance club to get out, saw him hit that girl on set, but he's never laid a harsh finger on me. Thing is, things change.

I brought up his whereabouts the last few nights tonight and Donnie's face got so tight I thought it would implode. He didn't say nothing at first then he reared back and got me good across the cheek.

Thing is, Donnie didn't hit me hard. I wasn't bleeding. I knew he was holding back. I knew he was fighting the urge for a long time because again, he has anger problems. I know that and I been known sense being with him. I'm fine though. I'm all good.

***

Today we shot a brother-sister scene. I did my job as usual, watched Donnie do his. After the shoot Donnie apologized, said he'd make it up to me. I thought to say don't worry about it, but I consented instead. Sure, I thought, he can make it up to me.

***

Donnie and I went to dinner at a nice restaurant for a change. I ate shrimp, fries and salad. I was so full that I had to sit awhile and think my thoughts through. Donnie said he wasn't through with me. He told me to not get dessert. Said he wanted me to not be bloated for the bedroom. It's funny, I was thinking about the bedroom too.

***

After eating out, Donnie took us home. During his second meal I realized how poor his tongue skills were. Staring at the blackness of the television reflection I thought about life as it was, the after of this moment. Then we had sex.

We passed out on the bed staring at the ceiling. Both of us were full and fat. Time passed a bit. I felt myself actually age in the bedroom. Felt the wrinkles etch across my face. My body was changing and I couldn't go back.

Donnie apologized again, said something about movie making, but my mind was already elsewhere. I told Donnie I wanted to do something for him. I told him I had something for him, but he'd have to wait. He smiled and asked what it was. I told him it was surprise and shut off the lights.

***

Today was an orgy. One of the new girls on the block filmed a scene. Apparently she was the one Donnie was seen around town with. He must have been negotiating. That's my Donnie, business minded. After the scene he pulled her to the side when he thought I was talking about

51

food with the makeup girl. That's my Donnie, always dumb.

***

Tonight was my night to treat Donnie. I cooked him a pasta dinner with spring rolls on the side and gingerbread cookies fresh from the store, but warmed up nice in the oven. I didn't eat much, I wasn't hungry.

***

I never got into the fetish of bondage. To me, being bound is the stupidest thing a person could actually want. I don't care how much you trust a person. You should always avoid anyone tying you down. To be tied down takes away every bit of agency and resistance. You can't resist, you're in the hands of another.

I don't care if sex is involved. I don't care if you've been married for twenty years. Avoid bondage, you can't trust people. I got to the point where I couldn't trust Donnie anymore. So I got him undressed and introduced part one: eight pairs of handcuffs from the local sex shop. Let's just say I know a girl who knows a guy.

Of course, being a red bloodied male, Donnie willingly accepted being cuffed and blindfolded. I interlock two pairs for each limb and secured the cuffs to the bed frame. It was perfect. I insured Donnie the handcuff keys would be on the nightstand, and they were. After some teasing I stopped and pretended to forget.

"What wrong?" he said.

I told him I forgot something and needed to fetch it before the fun started.

He didn't protest. He just said, "hurry back."

52

I left him in the room naked, blindfolded, handcuffed, with the handcuff keys on the nightstand. Then, I went to the garage and got the gas can.

***

Farrah was on my mind to and from the gas station. I was calm while driving, which is funny because I hate driving and it was night time and I was a woman alone, but I had no fear. After leaving the station I parked outside the house and took the gas can inside. It was time for part two.

I went upstairs and, as expected Donnie, was still cuffed to the bed. His penis was flaccid, so I teased it a little to get the blood back in the right place.

"I'm ready!" he went. "I'm ready!"

And Donnie was humping the air like an invisible woman was in the room and had just climbed aboard the meat train. And I was staring at this man, who I actually loved, the man I thought I'd be thanking on award night, when I eventually won something for a role in some independent film without Hollywood backing. I was staring at this man for a good while, watching his excitement bounce, watching his tongue waggle, watching his balloon belly sway this way, that.

Then I was around the bed, minding my shoes.

***

It's morning. The road is so lovely in the morning. I'm driving and I know where I'm going. The house, the industry, Donnie, I'm leaving it all behind. I only took a few things. I need a fresh start. The past is a blur, I don't respect it.

53

Hollywood is far away, but that's all right. I'll get there. I know how to travel and I don't mind traveling alone. I've been doing that anyway. I've been traveling to a dream in my head, now I'm doing what my mind wants.

I'm even thinking about changing my name. Every actress needs a Hollywood name. Maybe I'll be Marjorie or Francine or whoever I want. I don't have to be bound to myself anymore. I don't have to be bound to Donnie anymore. I can be whoever I wanna be.

I look up to Farrah, but I don't look like her and that's okay. I don't have her hair or her skin or body type, but that's okay too. I'm myself and I'm good enough. I'm enough of a person not to be stuck. I'm enough of a person not to be struck. I'm a good person and a good actress.

I'm gonna show the movies how good I am. I'm gonna do right by me. I'm sick of pretending to be okay. I haven't been. I've been complacent. I'm done with that now. I'm a new woman and I'm getting something that shines. Farrah will see. I'm making her proud. I'm leaving the flames behind.

The Gumshoe and the Glitterati
(Rie Sheridan Rose)

The phone on my desk jarred me awake like a live wire to the gonads. The sun slanted low across the oaken surface, throwing alternating bars of light and shadow as it peeked through the blinds.

I blinked in surprise. Usually, I was up by noon. I reached for the phone and knocked an empty Scotch bottle to the floor. Whoops.

I fumbled the phone to my ear. "Tom Hannigan."

"Mr. Hannigan...I need to talk to you." The voice was breathy, sexy and 100 percent female. I recognized it by the way she said my name, but I was more used to hear it cooing "Tommy, don't stop..."

"What is it, Louise?"

"Come to the apartment. It's urgent."

I sighed. "Again?"

"It's different this time, Tommy. Honest."

I looked at the clock over the door. I might as well humor her. After all, she'd been my client—in more ways than one—for several years now. My only steady client and the source of most of my drinking money. She was a society dame through and through and I didn't know quite what she saw in a broken-down loser like me, but I've been told I clean up pretty good. So, when Louise said jump, I usually did.

"I'll be right there."

I checked my snub-nose to make sure it was fully loaded. Lord only knows when you are dealing with Louise Templeton—she's as likely to shoot you as to kiss you. She'd done both to me—but swore the gun had gone off by accident.

By the time the taxi dropped me off in front of her door, I had a hundred reasons why I shouldn't be there and only one why I should. She was my girl. Sort of.

Because of that, I had hurried right over, wondering what the dame had gotten herself into this time. If it wasn't one thing, it was another—always something, and usually bad.

I rang the bell, the door flew open and Louise threw herself into my arms, sobbing like a chorus girl with a broken ankle. I patted her back automatically. This was gonna be one of the damp days. Well, at least I preferred it to the fire and brimstone.

"There, there, Dollface. Why don't you tell Tommy all about it?"

"Oh, Tommy—Rico's back in town!"

Rico LaCosta was a Cuban club owner with an eye for the birds and enough dough to make most of them sing. He'd taken a powder a few months back when the heat got to be too much. I wondered whose palms he'd greased to get back here so fast.

"What's that to you, Lou? I thought you and Rico were done before he left."

"We were... but I was the one who fingered him to the cops, Tommy. What if he finds out?"

I could see why she was worried. Rico had a dozen goons who followed him like puppies. One word and they'd rub her out without thinking twice about it.

"So maybe this would be a good time to take that trip to Paris you're always yammering about."

"I can't go away, Tommy—my sister's getting married in Fresno and I'm her Maid of Honor. If I were to ditch the wedding, my mother would have my head on a platter. I'd rather take my chances with Rico."

"So why don't you?" I asked as she dabbed her eyes with a little piece of lace that didn't look like it could do much drying. More likely the tears would just pop through one of the holes in the thing.

She didn't like that idea—spinning away from me and stalking to the other end of the room. "Rico wants to dance on my grave. He's put a hit out on me, I'm sure of it."

"I ain't heard nothing about that."

"Well, no one would tell *you*, would they? Half the town thinks we're an item."

Including me, most days. "We ain't?"

She laughed with a bitter, brittle sound that sent ice through my veins. "Sure, we've had some laughs, Tommy, but we'll never be more than that. Can you imagine?"

Well, yeah. Yeah, I could. And most days, it seemed like a pretty good idea. *Today*, it had seemed like a pretty good idea. Otherwise, why the hell would I have come?

"What do you want me to do about it?" Suddenly, I didn't much care—but maybe she'd at least pay me enough for rent if I was sympathetic enough.

"Isn't it obvious? I want you to rub him out." Her eyes glittered like two emeralds over her heaving bosom. She was nearly panting with fury. "I want him dead!"

"I ain't no hit-man, Dollface."

"I'll pay you twenty thousand dollars."

For that kinda lettuce, I'd become a rabbit.

"So, maybe I can learn."

***

57

The cab ride across town to Rico's place gave me time to think. If Louise was willing to give me twenty large for icing Rico... what would he offer for me to reverse that? Like I say, we'd had some good times, Louise and me—but apparently I was the only one of us who thought we had a future. On the other hand, someone like Rico was always looking for some extra muscle.

If I told him Louise's offer, would he be more likely to shoot me or counter her terms? He was a businessman and she was a dame—beautiful, sure, but beauty don't pay the bills and an ongoing income trumped twenty thousand any day.

A pair of apes in tuxes came ambling over as I stepped out of the taxi. I saved them the trouble of frisking me by pulling my snub-nose out of my coat with two fingers.

"Not looking for trouble, boys," I murmured, handing the snub-nose to the nearer of the gunsels and then putting my hands up to show I wasn't dangerous. "Just want to confab with Rico about something."

They put their heads together, spitting out Spanish like dueling Tommy guns. Finally, the bigger one gave a little bow. "Come with me, *por favor*. I will take you to Señor LaCosta." His English was heavily accented, but his grammar was better than mine unless I was making an effort.

I nodded and followed him into the club. His partner moved in behind me and I swear I felt his breath on the back of my neck. I couldn't shake the image of a shiv sliding home between my ribs.

Despite the prickle of the hair at the back of my neck, I made it through the building alive, to be shown into Rico's opulent office. It had a wall of glass overlooking the dance floor and the heavy beat of salsa music reverberated the panes.

Rico stepped forward, hand extended. We'd met a couple of times at various functions—usually when Louise needed some arm-candy—so I felt confident enough to reach out and shake his hand.

"Always a pleasure, Rico."

The bigger guard whispered something in his boss's ear and Rico tilted his head to listen. His eyebrow raised. "So, Señor Hannigan, Pablo tells me that you have something you wish to discuss with me."

"Yeah." I filled him in on Louise's plan and her proffered payment. "So, you see, Rico," I concluded, "I thought it only right I give you a chance to give me your side of the story."

"My side of the story and what... thirty thousand? Fifty?" He shook his head with a little sigh. "I am sorry to disappoint you, Señor, but the truth is, I plan on returning to Havana within the week. I only stopped by the city to clear up a business matter. But I do thank you for apprising me of Doña Louisa's irritation with me. I can't let that go unanswered. It would be terribly impolite and, in our circles, as you can imagine, that simply isn't done."

He whipped a gold-plated revolver out of his waistband and fired before I even realized he'd done it. White hot heat ripped through my gut and I fell to my knees on the crimson carpet.

"I so appreciate this carpet, don't you, *mi amigo*? So much easier for hiding the blood, *verdad*?" he said to Pablo, watching as I slowly toppled to one side. "When he is dead, take the body and deliver it to Louisa's front door. I wish there to be no mistake as to the meaning." He hunkered down beside me and murmured, "No woman is worth dying for, *tonto*. I am sorry your greed has taught

59

you this lesson too late. If you had merely brought me warning, we would both have profited... instead, Louisa loses her champion, I lose my favorite carpet and you lose your life. Only one of these things cannot be replaced. *Adios*." He patted my cheek as one might a child, rose to his feet, and strode out of the office.

I couldn't help but think, as my eyesight dimmed, how different things might have been if I'd fallen for a waitress instead of a society dame. Just goes to show... opposites might attract, but that doesn't make them good bedfellows.

The Case of the Cold-Blooded Killer
(Dona Fox)

The man's hands were rough as he grabbed at Eleanor's arm. She managed to slip from his grasp as she spun to the once shiny waxed floor, now dull with the dirt of the trampling hordes. No one offered assistance.

The glassy-eyed bargain hunters flowed around the struggling pair as if Eleanor and the big man were simply unremarkable rocks in the violent sea of their shopping surges.

The crystal chandeliers blinded Eleanor as they were surely meant to do while the tinny music of the piano threaded around her tongue and between her words until the man with the rough hands didn't possibly understand what she struggled to say—*'I'm trying to find my son!'*

Her baby must have crawled out of the stroller. And where had the stroller gone? Had one of those women who were following her spurting perfumes—and who knows what else—into her face had they taken her child? Their incessant spraying possibly meant to distract her— babies were worth money you know.

No-her baby had grown up. He lived up in Seattle-a big deal CEO. He sent her lots of money but no time to talk to his mother. Someone else owned his days and his nights. Not a minute for the woman who'd given her life to him.

She could have done a lot with all those years if not stuck in the house with a baby then a teenager—during the years when she had a figure and a face not yet fallen.

But this large fellow who could he be? He'd grabbed her arm and knocked her down. The knee she had landed on would hurt tonight. She'd have to ice it while she had her Earl Grey and watched her shows.

The gentleman wore a badge; maybe he would help her if she could unjumble her thoughts and words. But he pulled her coat off then slapped handcuffs on her while big eyes grew larger all around them. He pushed her into a tiny room barely able to hold a table and two chairs—one on each side. Interrogation followed.

She found herself again as he read her name and address to her from her driver's license. Her description and there—possibly a mistake in her age? Noticing the camera in the upper corner of the room; she straightened in the little wooden seat.

"Give me my coat and I'll go home now if this foolishness is over." She tossed back her head and thrust up her chin for the camera only then realizing she'd been handcuffed to the chair.

"What the hell?" she said, though she rarely swore. "What are your intentions?"

***

Earlier, Detective Aubrey lumbered behind the old woman as she darted from counter to counter, peering around and under every display. The saleswomen backed away rather than get involved except for the oblivious perfume girls with their incessant spraying—every time she came by they hit her again and she jumped.

Aubrey waved his arms through the mist and growled. They giggled and spritzed him again.

The woman muttered something as the detective edged closer.

"Where did I leave the stroller? Quentin will have my head this time. Did I bring the baby? Did I leave him at home?" She paused to run her pale fingers through her silver hair and he caught her; unfortunate she'd fallen down. He hadn't meant to be so abrupt and awkward; but clumsiness had always been one of his curses.

Once he had her in the little room Detective Aubrey emptied Eleanor's coat pockets onto the table; fancy lingerie blossomed in a colorful pile as if a thousand glossy butterflies were waiting along with Eleanor to take flight from the dismal room.

"Sir! I don't know how those abominations got in my pockets. The perfume girls were closing in on me crowding me; they may have slipped them there thinking to follow me out and retrieve their stolen goods later in the car park. I can pay for everything easily. I have money. My son has money." She blew on the pile and her breath moved a few garments to the side. "Why, they aren't even my size. One-size-fits-all," she scoffed, "I've never worn one-size-fits-all."

"Don't you remember me, Eleanor? This isn't our first encounter. Not even our second. I'm sorry. I've got to take you in again." The big man looked truly sorry. Eleanor felt bad for him.

***

The Public Defender spoke quick and too low; her voice not clear enough for Eleanor to understand a word except for something about an unfortunate third infraction and 'three strikes' which seemed to be deadly serious.

"Excuse me. I don't understand. Please come back." But the woman had gone on to whisper to the next prisoner then on to the next—each one down the line nodded as if they had no trouble hearing her mumbled

63

instructions—if guidance is indeed what the woman whispered—Eleanor had no way of knowing for sure.

She peeked from under her fringe and saw what appeared to be the same offenders in the courtroom as her first and second visits. They were a strange bunch, most with dead eyes but some had quick shifty eyes that cast darting glances around the room as if they were looking to escape but every last one of them had filthy chewed off nails.

Eleanor briefly thought of starting a charity; she'd provide manicure kits to the jails. Then she occupied her mind for a bit considering how to overcome the problems sure to arise from the misuse of her well-intentioned gifts.

Each time the phrase 'three strikes' slipped back into her mind her heart clenched.

Eleanor tried to think of being in the courtroom as much like being in church with penitents sitting in the pews, forced to suffer through a long boring sermon. Except for the handcuffs and a horrendous orange 'dress'—though of course they'd outfitted her in pants.

She'd not dwell on the fact the cloth which now touched her skin had been between who knows what other or how many other criminals' thighs. She shuddered to think of what crimes might have been committed between those very legs. They must bleach the clothing between uses. Surely they did.

She had a very good imagination and she tried to bring it into full play in the courtroom - for instance the odors and scents of her fellow parishioners - didn't the air carry a hint of Chanel? And over to her right a bit of Armani? No? And the girl beside her rolling dirt off her cuffed hands in tiny cylinders behind her back-must be a new beauty treatment the poor dear hadn't had time to complete before the morning service.

The voices in the 'chapel' were sonorous. Eleanor tried not to listen to the words—many were not family rated and her ears were very sensitive— she generally stuck to PG viewing. Her system worked until she heard her own name, then a blush fled down her body beneath the horrid orange 'dress.'

She looked up. The silence bore down upon her. They meant her to answer?

"Not guilty," she croaked.

The whole room laughed. Had she not understood the question?

The judge stood and his voice filled the room. "We'll break for lunch until 1 p.m. Bring Mrs. Landerpoole to my chambers." He swirled in his dark robes and disappeared as if he had performed a magic trick—perhaps screwed himself into the floor.

An officer took Eleanor's arm gently—not like the rude man in the department store—and led her to a door hidden in the panels at the front of the room.

***

Eleanor sat stiffly on the cushioned leather of the chair in the judge's chambers. They were alone. The guard had removed her cuffs; she bit the inside of her cheek as she ran her still perfectly manicured nail along the intricate carvings on the lip of the ornate desk, embarrassed to look up into the face of the man who held her freedom in his hands. The sign on his desk read: Judge Bennett Moore III.

"Do you recognize me? What I wouldn't have given fifty years ago to watch you model the items you stole this morning!"

Eleanor looked up into the Judge's face and back down to the sign on his desk then back into his face. Could he be odd little Benny Moore?

"Not politically correct now—is it? I guess never—I take it back and I'm sorry. Ellie. Look at me. I'm letting you go with a slap on the wrist. I have worse offenders to deal with—"

He indicated the files standing on his desk "—much worse—unfortunately I'll have to let them off with a slap on the wrist too—'plea deals' some days those are the two ugliest words in the English language.

"Look here—I sketch the miserable bastards sometimes in poses showing what I'd like to do to them," he chuckled as he held up a yellow legal pad with violent drawings, "then I shred my doodles. But I never thought I'd see you again—those were the days—and nights."

Eleanor wondered what nights he referred to—they'd never had any nights. He must be unhinged.

"I've already had your clothing brought up here so you don't have to go down to your cell again. I have to go before I say-or do-something I'll regret." He chortled—not a pretty sound. Not at all.

He hit a button on the intercom "—fill out the papers. Let's get Mrs. Landerpoole released a-sap. And lock up the cases on my desk. I have my copies." He loaded a number of bulging expando files into his briefcase.

He laid several thin manilla folders on his desk along with the gruesome yellow legal pad then he pushed them toward Eleanor. "Take care of these three for me. Remember—I could recall your case on a whim. Put you away 'till you die of old age. Just 'cos I can't do it to these murderers," he pointed at the three files, "don't think I can't do it to you—no one's watching your case

66

like they're watching theirs. I'll pick you up for dinner on Thursday to check up on your progress."

He went out a door in the back.

Eleanor looked at her pile of clothing neatly folded on the chair at the side of the room and wondered if Benny planned to watch her dress through some peephole or a one-way mirror.

What the hell. She wanted out of here. She'd dress fast. Too bad she couldn't shower first. She would have to burn these clothes when she got home anyway no way she could launder the stench of this entire experience from them.

Eleanor dressed as quickly and modestly as she could then threw on her beloved coat. She could not burn her coat—not in a million years—the coat being the last thing dear Quentin had bought her before he was killed.

She turned back to Benny's desk and impulsively swept the three files and the yellow tablet into one of her giant pockets.

Eleanor closed the last button on her coat as the assistant entered.

"Let's get you processed and on your way."

***

Eleanor stumbled out of a side door of the courthouse into an alley, feeling a bit disoriented; from there she called an Uber. At that moment she couldn't quite remember everything that happened in court but finding herself on her way home everything must have worked out.

She certainly remembered the grimy jail cell she'd been subjected to so she built a fire and burned her clothes as soon as she got in her apartment. Then she took

67

a bath. After her soak she made a cup of Lady Grey tea which she planned to drink in bed.

She hadn't hung up her coat. How careless of her.

Her coat felt heavy. Why were her pockets so bulky now?

She closed her eyes as she pulled out three manilla folders and a yellow tablet.

Where had she picked those up?

The yellow tablet looked like the drawings a young boy makes in class to stave off his boredom. Torture and murder—and one racy picture which for all the world looked like the judge with his black robes billowing as he made love to some old woman. My goodness—the old woman looked rather like Eleanor!

The events of the last day rose clear in her mind and crushed her like a sledge hammer. Both embarrassment and fear twisted in her stomach.

Benny must have recognized her or saw her maiden name in the files before he called her into chambers; surely he didn't want to make love to every ancient female criminal who came into his courtroom. What kind of pervert had he become?

What I wouldn't have given fifty years ago to watch you model the items you stole this morning! I have to go before I do something I'll regret.

She settled on the floor in front of the dying fire and looked at the three case files she'd pulled from her pocket and matched them up to the drawings for each man. Benny wanted them murdered all in different horrendous ways.

Take care of these three for me. I could recall your case on a whim. Put you away 'till you die of old age.

Preposterous. This is to be the price of her freedom? Could she pull it off? A pretty big ask. Would it pay for any future mistakes or would she be given more files? More gruesome assignments. Awful bargains with the Devil.

I'll pick you up Thursday to check up on your progress.

Ridiculous. She wouldn't do it. Absolutely not. She put the files under her mattress and took three sleeping pills to ensure she wouldn't dream. Still young Benny along with Judge Benny and the murderous three chased one another around the bed as they dripped blood onto her heirloom hand knotted rug. They crawled across the irreplaceable Versace comforter, pausing only to breathe into her face and whisper, *'till you die of old age.*

Then Eleanor dreamt. In her dream she woke the next morning and she put on her best Chanel suit and all her finest jewelry and full make-up. Jonesing to go shopping. No. She couldn't. Didn't dare. Why not? She'd control herself. Keep her hands in her pockets. Wear gloves. She'd fill her pockets ahead of time so there'd be no room for anything else. There's the ticket!

At the department store—headed for the door—she felt all their eyes on her. She strutted to the door, positive nothing waited in the shadows of her pockets except her own scarves she had stuffed there this morning.

She drew nearer to the door and security closed in on her.

She felt the thin gold chain underneath her tongue. No. What now? Had she picked it up in jewelry? Truly? She'd done it again? The unfamiliar chain? She felt above her collar. Her own necklace still there. She roamed the store in wild circles and somewhere in the centrifuge she spit out the chain then flew out the door. Safe. Olly olly oxen free. Whew.

Eleanor woke drenched in sweat. It had been a nightmare nothing more—this time—but the dream had convinced her she couldn't control herself. She would shoplift again as soon as she got the chance. She needed a get-out-of-jail-free card.

"I'll pick you up for dinner on Thursday to check up on your progress." Benny's words came back to her; today—Tuesday. She had two days—and two nights—to become a cold-blooded killer. An executioner for the government. She would view her 'jobs' without emotion in a strictly professional way. The judge had sentenced them—his role in the system after all—she would merely carry out the orders of the court.

Would she?

No.

Yes. To save herself she must.

Could she? She had to. Eleanor could do anything she set her mind to; maybe.

Eleanor slid out from under the covers, dropped down to the floor beside the bed and pulled the folders out from under the mattress.

I'll just look at them as if I were going to...—she couldn't even finish the thought in her mind but she mustered a brittle-thin bravado as she mumbled, "which one would be the easiest? To cut my teeth on, so to speak."

She covered her mouth, unable to bear the sound of her own hysterical laughter. But she could not stop.

***

Wednesday morning Eleanor's resolution flagged once again after a full American breakfast meant to fortify her- instead it made her sluggish and she decided she

70

would not become a killer. Not for any reason. She put the files in a brown paper grocery bag and tucked it in the back of her closet.

She thought hard what to do with the revolting things; she would not leave them in her closet and she couldn't return them to the Judge and admit failure nor could she burn them. What if the men did end up dead—such men often did—and she somehow became a suspect? It could happen if only by her own awkward actions or the vibrations from her own guilty mind. Burning the files was out of the question; the police have ways of reading words in the char.

Thursday morning she woke up with a plan; she'd go out in the darkest part of the night so bundled up as to be unrecognizable and walk—she could not take a taxi (taxi drivers are known to talk for a bribe).

She'd find her way on foot to the farthest parts of town so she could dump the bag then the files in isolated trash cans, then she'd hike all the way back. Perhaps she could not discard the bag so simply as there was the issue of fingerprints and there might be some code to the store the bag came from hidden under the glued together parts on the bottom in the folds.

Eleanor bundled up and headed out. Fingers numb from the cold and only halfway to the first trash can—her phone rang. She looked at the screen. Benny—The Judge. She couldn't avoid him forever.

"It's Thursday. Did you forget our dinner date?"

"Oh my gosh. I did. Maybe another time. I'm not even home. I'm out walking."

"Where are you? I can pick you up."

"I'm not dressed for dinner."

"We'll go somewhere casual. We could pick something up and go back to my place? We can talk about your get-out-of-jail-free card." His voice was oily and suggestive.

"Not tonight. Give me an extension to the week-end. Please."

"Okay. You got it. I'll take care of a few things myself. See you Monday then. I'll pick you up after court."

***

Detective Aubrey watched Eleanor slip her phone back into her pocket then followed her as she ran back to her apartment. Glad to be in his car—he didn't know how she did it—he knew he couldn't handle this much exercise.

Her walk was awkward. The pockets of her black trench-coat were full. He sat outside with no dinner—just a stale piece of gum to ease his hunger—but it paid off.

Eleanor slipped out in the early morning with the pockets of her trench bulging and her silvery blond hair tucked under a dark scarf. Aubrey could see no hint of anything but dark clothes clear down to her shoes. He might have missed her altogether if not for the dim light in the vestibule shining on her bright face.

She chose to walk once again-although with much even difficulty this time and she consulted her phone at every turn.

***

Eleanor realized the danger of looking up the murderer's address on her phone but what else could she do? She didn't know the city by heart and she had no familiarity at all with what she thought of as the dodgy blocks.

She also took a chance and brought her own 'possible' weapons; what if she couldn't find any weapons to use in his home?

The file said since he'd killed his girlfriend the murderous bastard lived alone; unless he'd already found a replacement for the poor dead girl. Eleanor hoped he hadn't moved fast to find another but she'd deal with complications when and if they happened—the coward dies a thousand times the hero but once—somebody wise once said and Eleanor would need to repeat the mantra many times this weekend.

The lights were out at the bastard's apartment and the door ajar. Senses on high alert—apparently murder provided an adrenaline rush similar to shopping—Eleanor pushed the door open with the toe of her shoe then stepped to the side. She waited a moment, listening for a reaction or for any sign of movement from inside then stepped into the apartment.

She didn't commit the murder—when she went into the apartment the guy was already dead.

She once again imagined this sort of thing often happens to guys who live this kind of life—probably done in by a relative of the girl he killed. They must have gotten to him before she could. Made sense. But she'd better get out of there quick.

She ran. But something bothered her; ironically the bloody scene showed the murder played out exactly like the Judge envisioned it.

***

Detective Aubrey went into the apartment after Eleanor left. He surveyed the carnage. He was heartbroken. He kind of liked her pluck and now he would have to arrest her for murder. He followed slowly behind her. He didn't want to scare her and have her run off, rather he wanted to get her in her own apartment. But she headed somewhere else.

***

Eleanor opened the second guy's manilla folder then read about an awful human being - possibly the worst of the three. But smaller - he should be easy to handle and he really deserved it. A bully. Hurt his step-kids. Real bad. Eleanor didn't even want to think about it but her conscience ought to be clear afterwards.

Eleanor once again entered a murderer's house where she once again found a body—fresh dead—but this time the mother of the damaged kids was there.

The woman had tears glistening in her eyes and a huge smile on her face as she said, "the avenging angel made it right. He came like he said he would and cut the devil down. The angel kept his promise to take care of us. Now my babies can sleep in peace."

Now Eleanor was angry as hell.

She slipped out the back door and watched from the neighbor's side yard as Detective Aubrey went in the front.

"I'll call you in a bit," she whispered, blew the detective a kiss and called an Uber.

***

On her way to the third murder Eleanor called Aubrey and gave him the address where she'd be. She took an Uber this time, paying the driver extra to step on the gas.

A dark Mercedes was just pulling up to the alley behind the house. She had the Uber driver drop her down the block and she jogged up to the house, muttering 'a coward dies a thousand deaths' as she headed straight in the front door.

"Hello, Benny."

***

The Judge was wearing his robes. The man was kneeling on the floor in front of him— the 'murderer' wasn't dead yet.

The Judge held the gun out to Eleanor. "Put it to his head. You take the shot."

"I felt this one could be innocent. You should let him live." Eleanor put her hand gently over Benny's hand and the gun.

"He's not innocent. This is my court. I've ruled." Benny stomped his foot. "Put the gun in his mouth and point it upwards; he'll be a suicide in penitence for his crimes."

"Did you hear me? I believe he's innocent, Benny."

"He's been tried and convicted and I've sentenced him."

Eleanor grabbed Benny's wrists and pulled his arms up into the air. "You killed all these men!"

Benny took the opportunity to bring his arms down and put them around her waist then he brought his body next to hers. "You were going to if I didn't." His voice softened. "Tell me the truth, Ellie," and just as quickly his

75

tone became harsh. "Don't lie to me like you did in college."

He was confused. She'd dated Benny briefly but they'd never been intimate. She moved on to another man-the man she married. They became rich together and had a son, then her husband died—in a hit and run. And now she wondered about the identity of the hit and run driver who murdered her dear Quentin.

"I don't know. I'm not sure if I could have gone through with the murders," Eleanor said.

"You could have. Remember how you crushed me? But we could be together now." The judge caught her off-guard as he let the gun slip from his fingers and pushed her against the wall. His breath caught in his throat and the sweat of a murderer seeped through his clothing as he held her head between his hands and forced his mouth against hers.

She squirmed to get away and his body moved in response.

She bit his lips and he bit hers.

She screamed in his mouth and he screamed down her throat.

She scratched his face and he dug his nails through her clothing.

An earth-shattering boom shook Eleanor.

At the same time the Judge screamed and hot liquid splashed Eleanor's face and they both fell to the floor.

***

"The Judge will live. Just a glancing blow off his shoulder—all I could chance. Guy's never been hurt before so he couldn't take it. What a baby." Detective Aubrey put his coat over Eleanor's trembling shoulders.

"And the criminal. Why didn't he grab the gun when Benny dropped it?"

"He's on probation; he wouldn't dare touch the gun."

"Of course. I've learned some things from the television. I guess I've got a lot more to learn. Well. No. I hope you just witnessed my last foray into the criminal justice system."

"You know, Ma'am, you've got some problems but you're real sharp-I think you just need something to occupy your mind. Maybe you and I could work on something together. You know, get a little office. I'm ready to retire. I could offer to look into things for people? Help them out..."

"Oh yes! Do you have a pipe? Should I buy you a deer-stalker hat?"

"Hold on. Slow down. You'd handle the desk-the phone-the client files-nothing else. Understand? We can get you help for the shop-lifting thing—"

"My shoplifting thing would go away?

"I'll take care of it. I'm talking about counseling."

"Then it's a done deal! We'll be like a team?"

"Sure," he sighed, "if you swear to me, you wouldn't have killed anybody. Right?"

Eleanor laughed, "you, Sir, may call me Ellie."

Stage Crimes
(Olivia Arieti)

"It was one of your best performances, Judy, you sang divinely," Scott told his wife while getting in bed.

"You, too, did very well; Cavaradossi's role has always been a challenge for lots of tenors."

"Also the devil of Ralph managed to do a great job. Have to admit he's one of the best baritones we have nowadays, although I detest him."

That said, he turned out the light and his back to his wife.

Judy didn't add a word as she didn't want any follow up to the conversation. She knew that her husband suspected she was having an affair with Ralph, but he never talked about it openly. Perhaps something in the way she looked at him or in her tone when, during the performance, she promised to be Baron Scarpia's mistress which was too natural, too veracious and he'd spotted it.

She had been very young when she wedded Scott, an established singer who helped her climb the ladder. Fame was dearer to her than love and she accepted his wish to become his wife.

He had always been a very devoted husband and she did her best to be equally as devoted in a world where ties and feelings were regarded as stale and flirting was a common and exciting pastime.

When Ralph appeared on the scene, both in life and on stage, she couldn't help falling for him.

He was the prototype of the opera singer, handsome, gallant and romantic, not to mention the sensuality of his voice. The first recital was enough to win her heart and the many that followed consolidated their relationship that went beyond a casual affair.

Now Judy didn't know what to do, aware that Scott would never grant her a divorce.

The following afternoon she talked the matter over with her lover.

His living room recalled the setting of a bohemian attic with a fireplace, wooden table and chairs, candles placed here and there and a big red sofa covered by cushions with hand knitted covers.

"Looks like Rodolfo's place, honey."

"As long as you're my Mimì, I'd live even in the poorest garret. I can't think of my life without you, baby," and before she could reply, he kissed her passionately and led her to the sofa.

"There's only one way we can get married," she said while shifting his hand from her thigh, "You have to kill Scott."

Ralph gazed at her, "Hey, that wasn't in the libretto."

"Oh yes, it was," she smiled wickedly. "Better go through it again."

Then she got up, put on her coat and, before leaving, turned round, "Think about it, love."

The guy was as startled as dismayed. Judy was the only woman he had fallen in love with and he did have quite a few; but there was something about her that fuelled his deepest instincts with passion and lust. Her generous curves, her voice as melodious as the nightingales of fairy tales enticed him and he never had enough of her, but committing a murder was definitely too much.

"Well?" asked the soprano, entering his changing room before the performance.

"I can't do it, baby, I just can't."

"So you don't have the guts?"

"Say, you sound more like Lady Macbeth than Tosca, darling."

"Guess I'll have to say goodbye to you, sweetheart. Scott will find out sooner or later and might even kill me…" and added perversely, "you know how much he cares for me."

Judy struck the right chord. Fits of jealousy seized her lover along with a deep hatred for his rival. He would do as she said.

"I'm glad to see how much you love me," she whispered as soon as she found the right moment to slip into his bed. "You won't regret it, believe me."

The last performance of Tosca was within a few evenings and there wasn't much time to discuss the details.

"So I'm supposed to put real bullets in the rifles used for the execution, huh?"

"No worry, hon, that sort of mistake occurs in lots of shows, not to mention film shooting sets. Cavaradossi will die for real this time and I'll be prostrated by grief."

And that's what happened at the final performance of the opera.

After long investigation, no evidence was found and all cast was released from whatever charge.

Judy and Ralph went on working together, making love to each other, but waited a year before getting married in order to avoid unpleasant insinuations.

A few days before the wedding, the bride to be saw a bleak shadow in her changing room; it appeared again reflected in the mirror when she was taking off her make-up. She leapt up, terrified, turned round and saw Scott dressed as Cavaradossi, his white shirt dripping with blood.

'What a lousy trick is this?' she thought.

When she told Ralph about the lugubrious presence, he held her in his arms and assured that it had been only a horrible hallucination.

"You're worn out, sweetie, overworked too much lately and now with the preparations for the wedding you hit the top."

A new contract for recitals of Madame Butterfly in the country's most important opera house brightened her up. She would play the leading role and Ralph the baritone.

It was her big chance to become one of the greatest singers of her time.

Strangely, when signing it her hand was trembling... certainly due to the excitement, but just after the signature, the image of her husband in the blood dripping shirt appeared.

"Go away," she cried before the dismayed bystanders. Ralph quickly took her out and once again persuaded her that it was nothing but exhaustion.

"Leaving for a while will be good for you, darling, trust me."

The rehearsals began as soon as the couple returned from their honeymoon.. Judy was resplendent and her voice seemed to have benefitted from her new status. Ralph was as handsome as ever and always in good spirits.

Their criminal deed had left no signs in their conscience; guilt had been quickly replaced by pleasure and whatever regret was silenced; there was no time to recriminate on their unscrupulous way to fame.

Just after the premiere, Judy had the same hallucination; this time Ralph was worried and suggested she should see a doctor. Somehow he too began feeling uneasy about it and even annoyed.

His wife had grown tense, easily irritable and her seductive charm had vanished.

No better way to chase away all haunts than visiting other women. Adulation and flattery was what he needed most; soon the visits to his ladies became so intimate and frequent that he managed to rapidly dissipate all shadows.

When the final evening of Madame Butterfly arrived, both were extremely nervous. Scott's spectre seemed to pursue Judy and Ralph feared that some sort of punishment was in store for them.

Many were the impresarios and musical critics attending. The finale was expected to be even more successful than the other performances.

"No wonder we are so agitated," said Ralph, "just look who's out there. Contracts will be rolling in after tonight, you can be sure of that."

No audience had ever been more mesmerised, moved and horrified than the one attending the opera that night.

In the final act, when Butterfly stabbed herself with her father's knife, the blade penetrated her heart; a real weapon had replaced the false one. Scott's ghost stood before her, "You knew I'd never let that bastard have you; you are mine and shall always be."

Blood began flowing down the stage and hollow laughter resounded in all ears.

This time it was even more difficult to find the murderer and once again the case was closed without a culprit.

Ralph didn't cry much over the loss; somehow Judy's sinister halo had ended up disturbing him more and more.

He was sure that with her death the matter was settled...
Scott had finally got her back.

He couldn't know that the ghost was waiting for his
next interpretation of Baron Scarpia to obtain complete
revenge; the murderous knife would be used by Tosca
when stabbing the treacherous chief of the Roman police.

Regrettable Birding
(Rickey Rivers Jr.)

I saw a CCTV video the other day of a man chasing a woman around a supermarket parking lot. The woman was able to make it to her car and speed off before the guy caught up with her. The guy slipped on a bit of wet gravel. That's the only thing that stopped him from getting to her. That's the only thing that saved her, a bit of wet gravel.

Sometimes I think the universe can help us when it wants to. I don't believe in cosmic forces, but I do believe the universe is more powerful than we can imagine. You can be saved by the planet if it chooses to save you. Protection of the planet is vital. That's why these diets confuse me. You want to not eat animals, at the same time you recognize the ecosystem disruption of keeping too many predators alive, and there's always been items made from animal hides and horns. You can't stop advancement.

People confuse want with need. We've needed animals as much as they've needed us. We can take care of them, feed them, and they in turn take care of us, feed us.

Vegans and vegetarians are interesting. They're contradictions like the meat eaters they admonish. They talk of saving the planet, but don't practice what they preach. Access to better fruits, plants and herbs should be the ultimate goal of your movement, not throwing paint on someone for wearing a fur. It's a useless fight to go against your natural urges and the urges of people have been sex and meat for centuries. We love it. We crave it.

Not to say I don't indulge in various fruits and veggies, of course I do. I love variety, I crave that too. Life is about choices, mixture. One of the reasons people love the United States is because of its ultimate variety and mix of cultures. Not to say every culture gets along. It's nature to not get along with every single person, but we try to make it work. Likewise, meat eaters and their opposites can make it work.

We're in the animal kingdom. We're the dinosaurs after the dinosaur. We have yet to reach extinction. Why then, if we recognize that, do we fight so harshly with each other? I don't want to fight others, to hate others, but the world can push you in directions of want, of need. And of course, we all want to live well. Some prefer peace. Some would rather dance in chaos.

I keep thinking about the woman running from the man in the CCTV video. The imagery has stuck with me as a short film in the mind. I think of how terrified that woman must have been, being chased like that. What if she were the one to slip on the gravel? Wouldn't her end be tragic?

Women are so often sought after aggressively. They're treated like prey. When it comes to dating, that's exactly the plan. That's how so called self-help dating gurus address them.

"You are the hunter. They are the prey. Go out there and hunt."

That's the language, the words of a teacher wanting their students to become lions in the field of dating. The ultimate goal is vagina, or a relationship, take your pick. And you fail, of course, because failing is a part of the whole. You fail to succeed. But in that failure will be bits of glory, eventually you'll catch prey. This is the game of it. They say men love to chase after all, but that's a funny thing to dream.

Speaking of which, my dreams have been rather vivacious. Recently there was one featuring me tied down and whipped repeatedly by a woman with a cat o'nine tails. This dream seemed to bother me. In fact, I woke up stunned, confused and actually quite aroused. I covered myself, my shame, my erection. No one else was there, but sometimes the mind craves embarrassment too.

In any event, after an awkward trip to the toilet I sat on the idea of the dream. Whipped so harshly with a brutal weapon, skin on the back shredded in stripes like claws dug in. The whole experience, a brief luxury, in thinking of the dream I bothered myself and masturbated on the bathroom floor. Unsightly, I know, but all the same - adventurous. It felt as if the dream had awakened something within, something forbidden.

***

I enjoy the challenge of landscaping. Some say inside work is easier. I'd disagree, it's only different and we need our differences, don't we? I've worked both in my life. I've cleaned kitchens, bathrooms, banquet halls and I've mowed grass, edged lawns and trimmed hedges; variety, you see, the spice of life.

That saying itself is so interesting. I wonder its origins. A truer saying must surely exist, but I find myself coming back to that one again and again. Every time I consider a different looking person I think of the saying. I've seen people holding hands who look strange to me, different cultures, sexualities and every time the saying seems to come back; variety, the spice of life.

It truly is. There was a time when I didn't use the saying, a time when I was less than tolerant of different looking people. You see, I was raised that way. To believe skin color determines your place in life, your standing in the grand scheme, these thoughts were not my own. My parents were terrible people. But we can't blame our parents for everything, only some things, sometimes.

And sometimes I think of the stories my grandfather told me about how things were back when he was a boy. How he had once saw a public hanging, how the image stuck in his head. I remember seeing his eyes glaze over. I remember grandfather nearly crying, to imagine a boy seeing such brutality at a young age. It's terrible and tragic, yet history doesn't care for empathy. History is cruel, all of it ugly, every triumph glazed with brutality.

I wonder if my historical connection with violence has brought about strange dreams of being brutalized by a barbed weapon, or is this connection merely nothing but the wants of a man? Do I wish to be brutalized, traumatized? Am I asking for redemption for some sin? I wish to say no, but I have sinned, as we all have sinned, but punishment for the sin, that is the question. Where does it start and where does it end?

I've consulted a dominatrix.

***

The online world is anything and everything, so it only made sense that I would stumble upon a dominatrix in my area: Mistress Guile. After a phone call we met at a secluded location before I could trail her to the dungeon. A makeshift dungeon is quite impressive once you're in the thick of it. Musty as it was, I felt something below walking past the chains and harnesses.

Mistress Guile was a sight as well. I'm not sure if a description would suffice, as they all seem to have a look, you know it: dark hair, leather, eye shadow, etc. To describe a woman is funny thing. They're often described like meat. Which cut is your favorite? You like legs, thighs, breasts? You want white meat, dark meat?

Regardless, Mistress Guile and I had a sit down talk before everything started. She asked what I liked, how I wanted to be treated. But I had questions for her first. I asked if a whipping fetish made sense. She said, "sure. Lots of guys like to be beaten."

I said I'm sure, but that's not what I meant. I specifically wanted to know if she'd heard of the fetish of whipping so roughly the skin is torn off the preverbal bone. And Mistress Guile gave me a confused look. She told me that she wasn't into blood play. Which is interesting, I didn't mention blood. She then said as long as I'm paying she'd do nearly anything to get me to the level I needed.

I asked to be beaten with a cat o'nine tails and had to explain further. You see, Mistress Guile didn't carry the particular whip because the type was banned and had been banned for a long time. You could only find knock offs now. The type I wanted tore flesh and again, the Mistress swayed from blood play. Something I never said or wanted.

After further discussion we settled on a braided bull whip for my first and final session. Final not due to the Mistress, but final due to me, you see, the whip was the problem, not the woman. It's never the woman, as the dream woman had a particular weapon of choice. The session went smoothly, as smooth as domineering can be. The mistress mocked me during the session, called me names in hopes to achieve a level of absolute pleasure. Alas, no amount of mocking aroused me.

I was flaccid at the end of the session. I was disappointed, again, not the fault of the mistress. Mistress Guile was even impressed, tired.

"Most men can't take it."

I shrugged off this compliment as I was frustrated. I had wanted release. I thanked the mistress after payment and went on my way.

"Next time," she said, "bring a towel."

My back was shredded. I was a mess.

***

It took me a while to recover. In a state of misery I masturbated on the road. I wanted some kind of pleasure from the experience. With eyes on the road and the mind elsewhere I thought about the woman in my dream, how much she had punished me and in my thinking of this dream woman my erection had become so prominent that it begged me to release it from bondage. I did so and made a mess of the steering wheel.

I'm honestly not ashamed. It's a human right to gain pleasure, no matter how brief, however you can. I'm not ashamed. After cleaning the steering wheel with wet wipes I went home and directly to the shower. My back was bloody. I had to throw the shirt in the washing machine. A cold wash works well for blood.

***

I spoke to Mistress Guile again. I wanted to apologize for not being a better client. The Mistress told me the contrary; I wasn't as bad as some of her first timers.

I had to cancel any future meetings as I didn't want to get addicted to physical punishment. Mistress Guile said she understood and I asked her if it were possible for me to punish myself when I felt the need to. She said sure again. She said a cheaper way to punish myself for misdeeds or inadequacies was to lock myself up in a cage, treat myself like a dirty animal that didn't deserve care or respect or even food. Just lock myself up. I wanted to pay her for this advice. She said: "You know where to find me."

So I took the advice of the dear Mistress and bought a cage for myself. Then, of course, I put the cage where it belonged, around my private parts. You see, that is the ultimate punishment, to be denied the pleasure of release, able to be aroused yet not able to find relinquishment. I should have had the cage in her dungeon. Then possibly, I would have been as aroused as the woman in the dream had made me. Who knows?

I know who knows, but she doesn't exist. Only other women exist in my head: dates, family, the mistress and a particular girl from back in the day. High school is a terrible time to teach anyone anything. So much was left behind in the classroom. It's a place for the future to possible excel. It's a place for the future to also fail.

I had friends in school, but none of us were 'cool', so to speak. Then again, what is cool really? Honestly, who remains cool throughout their life? Cool is temporary, a moment in time. Anyway, none of my friends then mean anything now. All of them are living their lives elsewhere and that's good. I don't have a particular urge to meet any of them in the present. In fact, I hope they're doing well.

Beyond them is another who I hope is doing well. Her name is Penny McDowell. She and I were in several classes together from 9th to 12th grade. It was only in 11th grade that I had noticed her eyes on me. However, those eyes, which were dangerous, were not only on me. If only I had acted soon enough we could have actually been something of a couple. If only I had been braver a person. Then I wouldn't be led to this fetish. Then I wouldn't be led to a cage. But a cage is what I deserve.

I'm not good, none of us are. The idea of good and bad is ridiculous. Regrettable choices are a constant. Animals even regret choices. That's why pet owners punish them.

"Good dog, bad dog."

It doesn't matter if you strike a dog with each statement. That dog will be confused, not know whether it's being good or bad, as if the dog knows a decision is a decision, a choice is a choice. It's a choice to strike an animal, to strike a child. I made a choice not to ask out Penny McDowell. But that wasn't the only regrettable choice.

Word had gone around that Penny slept around. It was something that didn't necessarily bother me because I still liked her. To me the rumors were only rumors. They didn't matter in the grand scheme. I still liked her smile. I still liked her hair, her long socks which reached her knees, her everything. Penny was a crush and you don't find flaws in crushes.

Regardless of my unwillingness to accept fault in Penny, the rumors persisted and they had gotten to her. I had once seen her crying in the gym, just crying alone. It's not that she didn't have friends, but even she wanted time to herself, as anyone needs. But I was a dumb teenager then, I didn't pick up on obvious things.

I went to her, and simply said "hey, Penny." It was the only thing I could say, a small greeting to a classmate. Penny looked up from her tear stained hands and saw me.

She just said "hey" but her voice was dead. She was there, but cracked. I started up the bleachers, just to get close to her, but she raised a hand and said, "leave me alone."

So I did, I left Penny alone. I never said anything else to her. Of course, she was upset. High School rumors can ruin your life. At least it feels that way at the time. But her life wasn't ruined to me. To me she was still Penny, pretty Penny with the bouncy hair. I still liked her. She was still my crush. I never wanted to see her crying like that again. But what could I do? Punish the whole school? Imagine if the rumors were true.

***

One of the last days of 12th grade was the day I saw a scene that sticks in my mind. On that day I was walking the halls. There's not much else to do towards the end. At the end you're done. You don't need to worry about grades or teachers or bullies or rumors. It's the end. It's all over. You've survived.

Imagine my surprise, walking into the gym and it being quiet except for a small noise from the boy's locker room. Imagine my surprise, walking into the boy's locker room and seeing Penny on the shower floor with three guys; a guy on either side of her, their legs on her arms, each guy holding a breast, a leg, another guy standing over her and Penny with tape on her mouth and tears in her eyes.

Imagine my surprise at this scene. I'm standing there in the boys' locker room and I see her being held down. She's struggling. She sees me looking and she's crying. And I know by reading her eyes she wants me to help her. I know this. One guy turns and looks at me. Then the other guys look and Penny's still begging for help through tears and struggling to scream through muffling tape.

One of the guys says, "Be cool."

Another guy says, "You want in?"

And I'm seeing Penny's panties hanging on one of her beautiful legs. There's a stain there. I still remember that stain. I had no words. All I could do was untuck my shirt and take off my pants.

Get Yourself A Hobby
(Diane Arrelle)

"Get yourself a hobby."

Edgar stared at the doctor. "A hobby?" he snapped, "I don't have time for a hobby!"

The doctor chuckled humorlessly. "Do you have time to live? Well, not if you don't slow down, perhaps even retire, and find something to relax you. Edgar, you are going to die if you don't learn to control your stress."

***

Edgar shook the memory of the doctor's words away like a dog getting out of a bathtub. It had been a year and a half since that conversation and Edgar was now feeling great. He leaned on the rake and surveyed the back yard. "Yep," he muttered. "Got myself quite a hobby." He smiled as he took in the neat stacks of firewood and the three huge piles of chipped wood mulch. "Quite a good hobby."

Martha wandered out to him wiping her hands on her gingham apron. "Come in, Dear," she said. "Have some lunch and take a nap. Then you can come out and finish the yard work. After it cools down a little."

Edgar sighed. "Yes Martha," he said and followed her into the house. No use arguing with her. She'd just get upset and remind him about the stroke. Even though he'd recovered fully, she still carried on like he was going to die at any moment. Hell, he'd even taken early retirement, just to please her. And, maybe because the stroke had scared him as well.

As he settled down on the screened-in patio, movement from the hostess caught his eye. A rabbit! A rabbit was eating the plant he had so carefully grown from a shoot, the plant he tended everyday along with everything else in his garden. Anger flared and he jumped up.

"Edgar, please! Sit down! Whatever is upsetting you?" Martha asked looking alarmed.

"A rabbit! A no-good, damned rabbit is eating my plants. Gotta go stop it!" he shouted and ran outside. The rabbit started and froze, then hopped off, only to stop a few yards away.

"Shoo…go away…" Edgar yelled, waving his arms and jumping from one foot to the other like an idiot. "Get out of here… NOW!"

The rabbit only watched him, then, as if bored with his antics, hopped to the next patch of succulent flowers, the marigolds.

Edgar couldn't believe his eyes; the rabbit was eating marigolds. The lady at the greenhouse told him to plant marigolds because the scent kept the rabbits away, and here the dumb bunny was treating the orange and yellow blossoms like a smorgasbord.

He felt his blood pressure rising and thought, a hobby huh, to relax! Hah! Edgar knew that in actuality, he was incapable of relaxation. Sure, he'd retired from the company he started and left with a pension and bonus to last five lifetimes, but he was a driven person, a real type A personality. Nothing wrong with that, except if you were prone to strokes.

He ran to the woodpile and hefted a small log at the arrogant creature. The piece of wood crashed down next to the rabbit, finally scaring him off. Unfortunately, it landed on several of the plants crushing them. Edgar ground his teeth together and swore. Nothing was going to ruin his garden. Nothing!

Martha stood on the back porch and he saw her wipe tears from her eyes. Damn that woman always made him feel guilty like he was letting her down. Well, he'd fix that tomorrow and went inside to take a nap.

The next morning after a stop in town to buy Martha a new diamond bracelet, and a special treat for the bunny, Edgar returned home and set about tending the trees he planted in the next field. He gazed at his property and felt proud of his small farm. Everyone had laughed at him when he left the company and became a farmer. But as he gazed at his saplings and recalled the mounds of chipped wood waiting to become mulch behind the barn, he knew he'd stumbled onto a small goldmine. He'd even discovered a new idea for a side business. The only thing that could ruin it for him were furry woodland intruders and he was ready for them now.

"Edgar, lunch time dear, then make sure you get that nap," Martha called in a loud voice from the house.

He sighed. They'd been married twenty-five years. She was a good, wife, a perfect wife, but she just wouldn't adapt to the 21st century and use her damned cell phone. He hit dial and said when she eventually answered. "On my way, Dear."

***

As they sat at the table eating a salad, he pushed the velvet box toward her and said, "Sorry, I lost my cool, yesterday. I saw that I upset you."

Martha smiled and opened the box and ohhed and ahhed at the shiny trinket. "Oh Edgar, you shouldn't have! My word, how can I wear something this special on

96

the farm." She took it off the silky pillow and slipped it on her wrist. "Well, I'll be careful not to get it dirty while I clean the kitchen."

After lunch and a short restful nap, Edgar went out to the flowerbed and was rewarded to see the little bunny caught in the iron jaws of the trap. The small furry creature looked so small and almost sad as it lay dead in its own blood. The trap had done a good job, nearly severing the bunny in two.

Edgar grinned and felt really happy, happy like he used to feel when he closed a big deal at work, happy like when his company participated in a hostile takeover. Hell, just plain old happy. Donning large plastic gloves, he picked up the rabbit and threw it in the chipper. Then he reset the trap.

After dinner, he'd met with success again. Another rabbit! He put that one in the chipper, reset the trap and went to bed confident that he'd get another by morning.

To his utter delight, he found a dog in the trap, a big shaggy thing that appeared to have suffered a while. He recognized it was the neighbor's mutt. Too bad, served it right anyway, Edgar mused. It had no right trespassing.

Martha walked out bringing him a fresh orange juice and screamed. He turned to see her drop the glass, tears on her cheeks. "Oh my god, Rocket!"

He thought, oh shit, I've upset her. "Oh Martha, I just found this dog in the trap. I'd set it for the rabbits. This is just terrible. I feel so bad for the poor thing."

She bent down and patted its head. "Poor Rocket."

He looked at her feeling puzzled. "How do you know its name?"

She looked up at him, "Rocket is our neighbor Larry's dog. I always carry treats for him when I take my morning and afternoon walks.

Edgar was startled. Martha takes walks? "When do you take walks?"

She stood up and sighed, wiping her hands on the apron she always seemed to wear since they moved from the city. "Oh Edgar, remember when we used to walk every day? Well, when you gave it up to work in the yard, I continued the strolls. After all, you have your hobby and I can't spend all day in the kitchen."

She left him to tend to the dead dog and went into the house. The dead canine topped off the load in the chipper and he wheeled the machine over to the newest plot of dogwood and Japanese maple saplings. Edgar turned it on and watched the spray of red refuse mixed with the wood chips to fertilize the trees and ground. He knew that if he could keep up his varmint collection, he'd have a bumper crop of trees to sell next spring.

His cell rang and he was amazed it was from Martha.

"Edgar, I'm going to walk over to Larry's with this pie to tell him how sorry we are about Rocket. He needs to know what happened."

He grunted something in answer, wondering why she had changed from her frumpy jeans and tee shirt into stylish pants and top. He wondered briefly if she missed their life in the city. She never complained and seemed to enjoy taking care of him. "I'll make her feel better about this whole Rocket thing and went online and ordered a state-of-the-art stove and oven. "There! She'll be overjoyed with that," he said and clicked the phone off.

***

Later that night Edgar thought about the rich red mulch he had created. It made him feel warm and happy. He needed to make more, but small rodents were too slow

98

a process and people would notice if family pets started disappearing.

The next morning while driving into town the idea smacked him in the head, actually it smashed into the side of the truck. The deer bounced off at impact and died on the side of the road. He hit the brakes and backed up to stare at the dead animal. His heart was pounding in his chest and his hands were shaking. He couldn't take a breath and for a moment her thought he was having another stroke. But after a minute or two, his breathing returned to normal and his heart, while running a mile a minute, no longer hurt.

Edgar drove on, went to the barber and told them what happened. The next twenty minutes were filled with several conversations about deer accidents, there so many of them. Everything became clear as he tuned out the town gossip mongers. Roadkill. On the drive back, Edgar stopped at his victim and loaded her onto the back of the truck. Hell, she'd fill the whole chipper.

He drove home and joined Martha for lunch. "Don't forget to take a nap, dear, she said and cleared the table. You need to keep yourself healthy for me."

Edgar nodded and went upstairs and rested, but his mind was spinning. He heard the downstairs door open and close. Looking out the window, he saw Martha, in a dress walking down the driveway. Poor thing, he thought. All the designer clothes in the world and nowhere to wear them. He went online again and booked a tropical vacation for the two of them for the next month and then ordered deer feed and traps. He was going to have an ongoing supply year-round.

He was back outside setting more rabbit traps when Martha came back up the driveway. She looked startled when she saw him working. "Oh, I thought you'd still be sleeping," she said fussing with her rumpled dress and mussed hair.

Edgar frowned. "What happened to you? Are you all right?"

She smiled and fluttered her hands helplessly. "Silly me, I put on this dress and heels and tried to walk to the nursing home down the road. I wanted to dress nice to deliver some cookies to the residents. Everything was fine until I tripped at the bottom of the driveway and fell down. I'm fine dear. Just a little shaken."

"All right," he mumbled already distracted by a patch of weeds.

She smiled and left him to his garden.

A few hours later the new stove and oven arrived. Edgar came in to oversee the delivery and smiled at Martha. "I bought this for you because you love your kitchen. Now you can spend all day cooking and baking!"

She looked stunned. "Oh, how well you know me, Dear," she finally said. "I guess I have my reading cut out for me tonight." She opened the instruction manual and sat down.

The next morning, he woke to the most wonderful smells. The counter was full of muffins and cakes. "Edgar licked his lips at the chocolate fudge iced cake and headed for it.

Martha cut him off, a cup of coffee in one hand and bran muffins in the other. "Here Dear, these are for you."

He nodded to the cake, "And that? Is that for me too?'

She laughed. "Silly man, you can't eat all those carbs and hydrogenated fats. I'd get arrested for attempted murder if I let you eat that."

"But—"

She pointed to an angel food cake. "That's for later. I'm taking the rest to some friends."

He nodded, starting to feel grumpy when he realized what she had said. "Friends? I didn't realize you had made friends in town. Good for you."

She sighed. "Oh Edgar, you spend all you free time in the yard, of course you don't know I have friends. I'd die of loneliness if I depended on you for companionship."

Edgar, frowned slightly, then said, "Well, Dear, I'm glad you aren't bored living out here. I can tell you have adjusted so well to country life. I know I have. Why I could live out here forever and never set foot in the city again."

She nodded. "I know, Edgar. I'm so happy you have found a happy place. When you are happy, I am too."

As he started off on the morning roadkill run in the truck, he thought about Martha home alone while he worked on his new hobby. He'd promised her that they would spend their golden years together, but he rationalized they were only in their mid- fifties, way too early to think about those golden years. And he'd tell her about the trip next month after dinner. That will make her feel loved and appreciated. Maybe he'd buy her a set of earrings for the trip.

After Edgar loaded the carcasses onto the truck bed, he drove home remembering his argument with the fertilizer salesman at the feed store. He couldn't believe how much they wanted for a bag of shit. And now he had the perfect answer to his fertilizing problems! He didn't need to spend a cent, just mix in the rich nutrients from the dead animals with some compost and branches and he had the perfect combination to grow his trees and plants. "Hell, I'll enter something in the county fair and then after I win, I'll sell my 'super secret-recipe mulch'. Bet I could make a bundle."

He grinned as he realized that he was on the business comeback trail. Why just bother with firewood, mulch and trees when he could go global again? He'd just take it easier this time, learn to stay calm. Yeah, it would be nice to be back on top of the heap. Maybe he'd even send that doctor a set of golf clubs or something, as a thank you for making him give up the company and move on.

Then he saw the sign. Coming Soon: housing and a shopping center of big box stores. Edgar knew his business was about to hit a snag because he saw the bulldozers lined up in a clearing. The construction team would be breaking ground soon on the new 150-unit housing development that was scheduled to go up where the woods were, right down the road. Edgar's frown deepened.

Then he smiled with a burst of insight. More houses meant more lawns and Sunday gardeners and that meant more local business. Sure, global was great, but local also had some advantages like becoming well known in the community, maybe dabbling in local politics, and if his product became popular enough, he could sell the company in a year or two and let them worry about the world.

The main concern was less deer habitats. If they became scarce, what would he do then. In the meantime, Edgar needed to increase his haul of dead deer. At lunch, after he told Martha about their trip, he mentioned the new development and stores. "There goes the neighborhood," he muttered and she nodded sympathetically.

"I need to hire some local help," Edgar decided speaking up without realizing he'd said anything. "More help will increase productivity. If I get enough done, I'll rent a warehouse and hire a company to design protective containers for the product."

Martha frowned. "What are you talking about? We came here to keep you alive. You're heading for another stroke if you're not careful. I told the lady at the grocery store how we'd come here so you could destress your life and now you 're stating up again."

Edgar laid his hand or hers and felt it stiffen. "It's just a hobby, Martha. Just a small endeavor to keep me mentally occupied."

"Are you crazy?" she snapped. "I called the doctor yesterday and told him about your idea of a destressing program. I mentioned the headaches, the high blood pressure readings you've taken when you think I'm not watching!"

He jerked erect. "You called my doctor without asking me?"

"I'm telling you now!" She snapped. "He prescribed these new pills. Start taking them immediately and hopefully we'll have you under control by our vacation next month."

He sighed. His blood pressure shot up for a moment, but he realized she was only doing it because she loved him. He took a couple of deep, relaxing, breaths and smiled at her. "You are right as usual dear. What would I do without you?"

"Probably be dead," she said and laughed.

He laughed as well. "Probably right at that."

They sat in silence a moment then Martha spoke up. "I know just the person to help you out. He's a farmer facing foreclosure. He lost his wife, the crop last year, his chickens died of a virus, and of course his faithful dog Rocket died, thanks to us. Now he's going to lose his

103

home. Give him a job and maybe we can help each other out."

"That guy who lives down the road, uh… Larry?"

She nodded. "I was just about to bring him this chocolate cake while you took your nap. I'll tell him to come over later."

He opened his mouth to speak but really had nothing to say.

"Fine, now go upstairs and rest," she said as she took off her dowdy apron and picked up the cake.

Edgar nodded and thought about how good Marth's legs looked in that skirt and sandals.

***

Edgar watched Larry spread the mulch after he had sent it through the chipper. A good guy. Too bad he can't manage money or his own affairs. He thought about how lucky he was to have Martha by his side. Poor dumb Larry had let his wife slip through his fingers.

Life had gotten more interesting since Larry came to work for them. Martha insisted that the poor slump eat lunch and dinner with them every day. She cooked wonderful meals and made the most exotic desserts that of course she wouldn't even let Edgar taste. He took it in stride since she did it out of love for him.

The only thing that bothered Edgar was he just didn't feel all that well. He finally called his doctor and was shocked when he heard that his meds hadn't been changed at all. "In fact," his doctor said, "I was surprised you missed your last two appointments. You realize that a man with your conditions shouldn't stop your follow-ups."

"I… I…" Edgar stammered and hung up.

What the hell!

He called for Martha but she wasn't in the house. Felling confused and worried, he picked up his cell and called her.

To his surprise she actually answered the call. "Edgar Dear, I'm in the back field with Larry." Then she hung up.

With Larry? What the hell was she doing with him and in the field. She never came out to the work area, the bloody mulch upset her too much.

His head was killing him as he stumbled out to the far tract of his property to see what was going on. There they were, standing together by the chipper.

"Martha!" he bellowed then noticed that she was dressed in a beautiful black outfit and wearing all the jewelry he'd bought her over the years. The trinkets he gave her instead of his attention and love.

She glittered in the sunlight and he thought, Damn, she looks ten years younger. Then he shook his head. It was hard to think and his arm and hand was tingling. He took his attention away from her looks and remembered the conversation with the doctor although it was getting fuzzy. Everything was getting fuzzy.

He watched Larry take his arm from around her waist her and they waved him to come in closer, to join them. Edgar stumbled; his leg was dragging a little.

"That's good Dear," Martha said. That's a perfect place for you to fall, see right there where your head will hit that rock."

Larry walked up to where Edgar was standing. He picked up the rock and hit him on the back for the head.

Edgar fell and Larry bent down to place the rock under Edgar's head right where he'd been struck. "That

105

was for Rocket," Larry said and stepped out of his line of sight.

Edgar's head was exploding in pain. Why hadn't they killed him, he thought. Why did they just hit him.

Martha bent down next to him. "Edgar, Dear, you are having a stroke. Why you doubled your blood thinners and blood pressure meds, no one will ever figure out. Maybe they'll think you were starting to suffer from early onset dementia, but whatever the reason you've overdosed some mighty dangerous medicines. Any serious bump will cause massive internal bleeding and since you fell and hit your head on this rock well you know, brain bleed."

He was fighting to hold on to his thoughts, fighting to hear and comprehend what she was saying.

"Did you really think I was going to give up my lifestyle forever to be your faithful servant. Did you really think you could buy me with presents? And by the way that stupid oven was just the most insulting thing."

She lightly tapped his cheeks. "Listen up, Edgar focus on me, Don't die yet. I've got a lot to tell you. I wanted to leave you but, although you swore you loved me, that prenup was ironclad. Who loves someone and makes them sign a prenup I've spent the last eighteen months talking to everyone in town about how worried I've been. I've been the prefect wife, and now you go and die on me anyway. By the way, don't you just love this outfit, I ordered it for the funeral. I do so look good in black."

His vision was growing narrow closing in on itself. He couldn't feel anything at all, and his consciousness was fading. I'm dying, he thought, sadness being the only thing he was aware of.

Martha started to get up, then added. "I'll be a proper widow, spend my time between here and the city for the next year or so, then I'll fall in love and marry the foreman you hired, Larry here. I'll be sure to cancel that stupid island vacation. Better a nice, long, winter honeymoon cruise with my new husband."

He heard someone turned on the chipper and as the red wood chips fell on his unblinking eyes and clogged his nose and mouth, he realized they were burying him under his bloody mulch.

"Don't worry," Edgar," Martha called over the sound of the machine. "We'll find you tomorrow and give you a real proper burial service. In the meantime, be sure to enjoy your hobby, Dear."

Huliawwa: the Man-eater of Torgal
(Shashi Kadapa)

The tigress waited until the man started climbing the steep path from the river. Then she charged with a terrific roar, tore off his head and dragged the body over the rocks and into the forest and fed. Villagers found the half-eaten limbs scattered and covered with voracious fire ants. Dwindling forests and rapacious hunters had forced it to become a man-eater. This was the 13th kill of the dreaded tigress Huliawwa.

The beginning

The spate of killings in the early 1930s rocked the Princely State of Torgal, South India. His Highness Shinde was the king and Yuvaraj, (prince) Narojirao was the heir. The prince had recently returned from England after his studies and was fired up with ideas of social justice.

Terrified villagers stood at the Torgal fort gates clamoring for protection from the tigress. HH looked over the balcony and at the furore and asked the Karbhari Minister Savant to find out what the problem was. Guards were asked to let the sarpanch – headman and a few villagers, come inside. Patil the headman bowed low and waited for permission to speak.

Minister Savant spoke to them. "Yes. people, what is the problem?"

"Maharaj! The tigress Huliawwa killed sarpanch Bhimya. Please save us."

HH asked: "Huliawwa tigress? Who gave it this name? Are you sure it is a tigress and not some bandits who want to steal your cattle and produce?"

"No. Maharaj. No human will kill, eat and dismember the body. Please protect us."

The minister commented: "Maharaj, the tigress is real. It has already killed many."

The story of the man eater

Patil, "About five years ago a young girl, Huliawwa, was brought to the Yelamma temple at Saundatti village as a novice handmaiden to serve as a devadasi - jogamma in the temple. Some of these girls are traded by depraved headmen and landlords against the wishes of the goddess and many are held against their wish. Huli in Kannada language means tiger and awwa is an endearing term for females. Huliawwa means a woman who is a tigress.

"Huliawwa was unwilling to become a devadasi so she resisted. The temple attendants beat and tortured her and got her ready for her first night with a wealthy landlord and his sarpanch. She killed the landlord, ran out of the temple and jumped off the hill on which the temple is built. She fell into the thick jungle surrounding the temple and died."

"What has this to do with the man eater?"

The headman continued, "Before jumping, she placed a curse that she would possess the body of a huli - tigress and kill evil landlords and sarpanch. Attendants searched for the body and found a tigress sniffing the blood and the remains. They managed to trap the animal and tortured and burnt her face, pulling out a few claws and blinding her in one eye."

"One day, the tigress escaped, after killing the keeper and some attendants. They say that Huliawwa has possessed the tigress's soul and that she is killing only evil landlords and the sarpanchs."

HJH turned to the Karbhari and asked, "Do you believe in this possession of a tigress? How does it know who is an evil landlord, a sarpanch or a farmer? Anyway, if only those fellows are killed, why are you people afraid?"

"Karbhari Sahib, one never knows who Huliawwa will kill next," the minister said, "Maharaj, the vast forests have shrunk. Villagers are cutting the trees to grow crops. Deer, bison and other animals are scarce so tigers and leopards now kill humans."

HH Shinde proclaimed, "I think this revenge aspect is a myth. Anyway, do not worry. I will hunt this animal."

The crowd bent in homage thankfully and returned home comforted.

*****

Young prince Narojirao Shinde spoke out, "Maharaj, it my right and duty as the heir to hunt this tigress. Besides, I have hunted often in the jungles and shot tigers and leopards. Please let me go."

He looked at the adamant prince and said, "So be it. Take my guide Huchappa, an expert tracker from the Byadar hunter community."

He sent a summons to the hunter who arrived quickly. Huchappa the guide bowed low to the Maharaj and the prince. It was apparent that he thought that the prince was a wastrel like many royal family members. He had come because he respected the Maharaj. The prince looked with doubt at the hunter.

Huchappa was lanky, had one deep-set eye that flitted from person to objects as he weighed the dangers they posed, while the other eye was blind. He also limped and did not wear any footwear. He was dressed in an old dhoti and kurta with a turban and with his old muzzle loader he certainly did not look like an expert hunting guide.

Yuvaraj looked at his father with doubts. HH raised his hand and said, "One eye, one leg and his muzzle loader are enough. Never, belittle a person because of his appearance or clothes. You have to win over the people with bravery and kindness. The hunt provides you this opportunity. Always listen to Huchappa as he has saved my life many times. He is not your servant but a Sahāyaka - assistant."

The Prince sets off

Minister Savant had made queries. He reported to HH and others, "Maharaj, some interesting news has come out."

"What news?"

"Maharaj, the farmers want freedom, liberty from the landlords and to own the farms they till. The landlords will not give the lands away and they enslave young. Tigress is the mount of many goddesses such as Durga, Yelamma and others."

"So?"

"Farmers consider this tigress as a sign that gods have sent her to protect and give them freedom."

The prince spoke, "I think we should liberate the farmers and the girls. What is stopping us?"

111

HH said, "Yuvaraj. There are several alliances, agreements that I cannot break. The landlords and the temple committee members are very rich, powerful and they will resist any such attempts.

"If you can kill or capture the tigress then you have won the right to impose new rules. Be very careful for you do not just hunt an animal but fight old traditions and superstitions.

"The tigress attacks with no warning and you will have to shoot very accurately in a blink."

He gestured to his attendants and handed over his favorite hunting gun, Holland and Holland 12 bore. "This is the best gun in this part of the world. Always trust and care for it."

Savant whispered, "As the prince, you are the overlord of all the sarpanch and landlords and could be the main target of the tigress. You may meet the tigress when you are not on guard and she will test you. Promise the animal about your intentions and pray to Yelamma devi."

Yuvaraj bowed to HH and they set off on their horses. First they prayed at the Bhutnath temple and sought God Shiva's blessings and then set off. The retinue followed with provisions and tents loaded in bullock carts.

***

After a few hours' riding the prince and Huchappa sat under a tree with the soldiers standing guard.

Yuvaraj said, "I heard that the landlords and sarpanch exploit the farmers."

"Yes, Yuvaraj. They are all bonded farmers who are in debt for life to the landlord."

"This is very sad. What do you expect me to do?"

"Liberate the farmers and the girls, Yuvaraj."

"We shall see. I have to kill the animal first."

***

The retinue set up camp near Maganur village where the animal had killed Bhimya. Villagers came to pay homage and stood with gifts of sweets and flowers.

After accepting the greetings and wishes, the prince waved them off. Attendants started fixing camp and the prince and Huchappa set off to the ravine where the man was killed. A village headman accompanied them and pointed out the tracks that ran over the steep path from the plateau to the river. River Malaprabha had carved a ravine and path through which it meandered onwards.

Huchappa looked at the paw prints then at the manner in which the body was dragged. He also noted the pieces of flesh carried over by the forest ants.

"Yuvaraj, the prints are less deep in the front right side. Two claws are missing. The rear prints are strong."

"Does this mean the animal is injured? We can easily kill it?"

"No Yuvaraj. It can still kill us without any difficulty."

Then he looked at the rim of the ravine that stood far above.

"The tigress was disturbed in her feeding. She is still hungry and waits for prey at the rim above. I can see birds flying away in alarm when they see the animal."

"What do you propose?"

"We will start a beat from the top and drive the tigress down to the ravine. It will come down and run through this spot. You can get it as she starts to climb."

113

"So be it."

The villagers were ordered to climb to the top of the ravine and scare the tiger down with drums and trumpets.

Some villagers picked up muzzle loaders, dynamite sticks, pot bombs or earthen pots filled with gun powder, axes, sickles, bows and arrows and anything they could lay their hands on. The village headman and landlords squatted at Narojirao's feet.

Some bonded farmers, shaking with fear, climbed up the ravine slope. Then they started beating their drums, shouting and screaming.

The tigress roared and slid down the steep slope of the ravine in a blur of yellow. One leap and she crossed the river of twenty feet span, scurried up the opposite slope and was gone.

The villagers first fell over each other and the prince in fear. They fired their weapons and threw fire pots that fizzled dead and none of the missiles hit the tigress.

Three people were injured with muzzle loaders' buckshot, one was shot in the buttocks by an arrow and scores of unexploded fire pots lay on the ground, emitting ominous smoke. One arrow had managed to find its way and strike a spot near the Prince's head and another near Huchappa's leg.

Huchappa pushed away the headman who held his unfired muzzle loader pointed at the prince's chest. The shot was a dud, though he was making frantic efforts to fire. Neither Huchappa nor the prince had fired since they could not get a clear shot.

Huchappa summed up the exercise, "Yuvaraj, these fools are a greater danger than the tigress. If we hunt with them we will either get shot or stabbed."

"You are right, Sahāyaka. From now on we hunt alone."

"Did you notice something, Sahayaka.? Only the poor farmers went to the hill top for the beat. The upper caste landlords did not go. Why were the farmers willing to risk their lives?"

"If they had disobeyed the landlords, they would have been driven off from the fields. Being a serf means giving your labor, mind and soul."

The prince and his team stayed for a couple of days and he visited the farms, sat in the bare huts of the farmers, speaking and listening to them. He was moved by their poverty, fear and misery. He promised himself that he would do something about their plight.

News came of a tiger sighting down the river and killing of a sarpanch who had gone to cut wood in the forest near the Saundatti temple. The prince decided to move to the place of the kill.

The Prince meets the tiger

The retinue rode on the Ramdurg town road, stopping to pray at the Sunnal Hanumappa temple to the monkey faced god for strength and then moved on.

After lunch the prince sat on bedding under a tree, cleaning his gun. River Malaprabha flowed gently on its journey. It watered the countryside, bringing fertile mud from the Sayhadri Mountains and deposited the mineral rich soil on the land. It gave life, it was life.

Green fields with specks of yellow reached to the horizon. A few farmers had ventured into the fields and he could make out distant figures beating the drums and slinging stones to drive away birds that fed on the grain.

The prince loved the land, the farms and the people. He smelled the deep musk earthy aroma that wafted from

115

the freshly tilled lands. This was his land, his people and he would do what it required to liberate them.

Huchappa had gone to speak with the retinue. The prince had a sudden premonition of danger, that something was watching him and he slowly turned his head.

The tigress had emerged from the bushes behind the tree and stood about ten feet away. It eyed Narojirao, not making any sound. His gun was not loaded.

They watched each other like two fighters sizing each other up. It sniffed, cocked its head and looked at him with its good eye. The animal was huge, about nine feet and the tail whipped sinuously. The face was about a foot wide and the height at the shoulder was about four feet. It opened its mouth to lick the lips and he could see the fangs were about four inches long. There were burn scars on the face and one eye was gone.

Narojirao could see that the front right leg was injured and two claws were stubs. Muscles rippled on the legs and shoulders as it shifted its weight. It could have charged and killed him in one swipe, but it kept looking, staring deep and hypnotically into his eyes. There was no saying if it would jump or retreat and the prince felt death staring at him. He decided to face the man eater, not flinching from its gaze.

The spell was broken by Huchappa who saw the tigress and, shouting loudly, ran towards them. The animal whisked its tail and disappeared in the jungles beyond.

***

Huchappa said, "Yuvaraj, it could have easily killed you. It did not."

116

"Yes."

"You are very brave, Yuvaraj, just like Maharaja."

"Maybe."

"Yuvaraj, what did she tell you."

"You are my Sahayaka. There cannot be any secrets between us. The tigress spoke in my mind of the defilement of forests and rivers and the great oppression that my people face from the landlords. She told me of the misery of the girls who are held in bondage in the temple. She told me to liberate them and do what is right."

"Yuvaraj, what do you plan to do?"

"Carry out her wishes."

"There is something else, Yuvaraj. She is pregnant."

"What! Then I will not kill her."

"She cannot be trapped. You have to decide if you want to save the tiger or the people she kills."

"The new plan is now to capture her and liberate the people."

The Leopard at Hoolikatti hamlet

Word quickly got around that the Yuvaraj had faced the tigress unarmed, looked at her in the eye spoke to her and emerged alive. When he started riding on the road, poor villagers prostrated before him, looking at him as their liberator.

Narojirao rode and pondered about his mission in life. He was a privileged prince and commanded people to serve him. He would never have to push a plow and drive a pair of oxen to till the field and never work for food.

'Did he deserve this pomp and luxury? About the tigress He could trick her into an ambush and kill her and the baby tigers she carried. Did he want to kill them?' Now the idea of killing abhorred him. 'Did he have the

117

power, will and command to overturn the century's old practice of zamindari and devadasi?' He looked at the horizon and prayed.

***

Huchappa tracked the spoor and, after a few hours of ride across hills, ravines and through the jungles they came to the hamlet of Hoolikatti. The village of a hundred souls had families of farmers, blacksmiths who fitted shoes on oxen and horses, potters and traders.

Irawwa was a farmer recently widowed and it was tough for her as she worked the farm and looked after her baby. She was bound to lose her farm since she could not make the payment demanded by the landlord. She would be thrown out or choose to become a concubine of the landlord - zamindar and his henchmen.

Yuvaraj rode through the farm and looked with scorn and disgust at him and then at the zamindar who was lolling in his armchair under a tree. The fellow got up and bowed when he saw the prince.

The Yuvaraj realized that for Irawwa, he and the rapacious zamindar were no different, exploiters of the weak. This hit him like a blow and he longed to lift his gun and shoot the fellow dead.

Irawwa had placed her baby in a sling and hung it on a bush while she worked.

As the Yuvaraj talked with the zamindar a loud cry sounded from the farmers. A leopard had emerged from the crops and was sniffing the sling and the baby. It was a tiny morsel for the animal.

The prince drew his gun, cocked both barrels and stood ready to fire, then hesitated. If he fired, both the baby and the leopard would die.

118

Irawwa did not hesitate. She grabbed an axe, rushed at the leopard and stood between her baby and the beast with her axe raised.

Only a mother could show this kind of bravery and no leopard could cow her. The leopard could disembowel her with one swipe.

The animal crouched ready to spring when the prince rushed forward, pushing the woman aside. It was just a slash away and even as it reared to strike he let it have both barrels.

The shot flung it away, shredded and broken and Irawwa picked up her crying baby, holding it to her chest.

She broke down, fell at his feet and cried, "O Brave Yuvaraj, I pray that goddess Yelamma grant you a long and healthy life."

The prince looked grimly at the zamindar and gave orders to see that the woman was not exploited. He gave instructions to his people to speak to her and if she desired, to be given a job and a hut at the fort and care for the baby. Well, this was one soul liberated.

On to the temple

News arrived that the tiger was prowling the deep jungle near the temple. Reports came of roars, grunts in the forests and of sheep and goats killed. No human was killed and the people helplessly let the animal continue on its rampage.

No one was ready to work in the fields. Cows were hurriedly milked and then roped in the cow shed with feed. If this continued, farmers would go into debt and sink further into the clutches of the landlords.

Yuvaraj and his team were clueless about the whereabouts of the tigress. She hid in the jungle, then

119

emerged to kill a goat or cow, drag the kill to a hideout and then remain quiet. She would again kill a100 kilometers away for her range was huge.

***

Narojirao and Huchappa took the small break to visit the devi Yelamma temple. They bathed in the seven sacred pools and later the prince offered gifts and prayed to the idol.

"Who are those women bowing down to us from the temple ramparts?"

"They are the jogamma's. They are bowing to you to save them from this evil practice of devadasi and liberate them."

Narojirao sat quietly deep in thought.

***

A messenger came running with the news that the tigress had killed Basya, the headman of Kadihalli hamlet. It had dragged the kill to rocky outcrop and villagers raised and alarm and drove it away.

The Hunt progresses

Narojirao and Huchappa rushed to the spot before the body could be removed. They argued with the wife and father of Basya to let the body remain where it was. Burial could be done later as the tigress would return to eat the kill and they could trap it.

The prince looked ahead at the green farms that extended to the horizon. On the right was the rocky ridge sloping down to the huge lake that the river formed.

***

Huchappa gave orders to construct a strong cage of iron bars and wood planks to be placed at the dead end of an arroyo. A trap door closed the cage when a weight was dropped. The cage was mounted on sturdy wheels and covered with tree branches.

The body of Basya was dragged along the floor of the arroyo and placed at the back of the cage. A rope was tied around his chest and an opening at the top of the cage was made for the body to be pulled up.

The trappers rubbed themselves with twigs and branches of the trees that grew around to mask their smell and climbed up the platform. They asked all other people to go away. A few refused to go, saying they wanted to serve the prince.

The full moon crept up the horizon and they watched the corpse. At about 1 am, the bushes near the corpse moved slightly. The prince prodded Huchappa and saw that the hunter was wide awake and gazing at the body.

The tiger hid in the bushes and sniffed. It gazed at the surroundings, the trees, its ears twitching to hear any noise. Then it slid out and approached the corpse, stroking the chest with one paw and starting to drag it into a bush. In the moonlight, they could see the tiger as it stuck its neck and the leg out. It would shortly settle on the kill and start eating.

The prince had a clear shot but he did not fire. He remembered the encounter with the animal and the babies she carried. The people who were hiding did not keep quiet. They loosened a volley of shots, arrows and spear at these dolts who had scared her away.

121

The Tigress is caught

Huchappa said, "She will come again. We should be better prepared."

The prince told his soldiers to drive away the people as trapping the animal was important. Dry tinder was kept on the top walls along the path. These would be lit and dropped as the tiger entered the path. A few pots filled with gunpowder were also kept ready.

The prince and his team waited quietly for two days and nights, crawling off now and then to finish their ablutions and have light food. They knew that the tigress was very cunning and she would smell anything suspicious. The corpse was stinking and they covered their nose and face with thick cloth strips.

***

It came on the second night. The prince was dozing lightly when Huchappa nudged him awake. The tigress waited in the shadow. Then she crawled forward, very slowly, almost flat on the ground.

Huchappa motioned at soldiers to keep quiet. The animal was now through the clearing and to the corpse kept at the back of the cage. It did not like the smell of the cage but the body was in the corner and she had to go inside.

She slithered to the cage mouth. Huchappa shouted and scores of fire bombs and dry kindle were lit and thrown behind the tiger.

Scared at the flame from the previous burning, the tigress instinctively jumped inside the cage. Huchappa dropped the weighted door and the animal was trapped. It struck furiously at the bars but they held. The roars and

122

snarls of rage could be heard in the temple a few miles away.

The prince signaled and his men pulled up Basya's body and closed the opening, before the animal realized that its meal had disappeared.

***

The Yuvaraj and Huchappa walked over to the caged animal. There was no one else as the soldiers were keeping away curious people.

The prince raised his gun and pointed it at the tigress, looking deep into her eyes.

A pull of the trigger would finish the animal. The skin could adorn his throne and bring him respect as a famous hunter. Huchappa watched him warily.

Narojirao realized that he could not kill the fine animal. He placed his gun in front of the cage and bowed low and spoke. "Huliawwa. We have wronged the people and you. Yelamma devi, Renuka Amma. Please forgive us."

The tigress moved near snarled and looked him over. Perhaps it remembered the last meeting it had with him. It sniffed and turned back to go to the rear part of the cage.

The prince picked up his gun and turned. Huchappa was standing very near the cage. His face was lit with relief as he looked at the animal and the prince.

***

Basya's body was handed over to the grieving relatives for burial and the prince gave them a grant of farms for their help.

A bullock cart with the side posts removed was brought and the cage was further reinforced and heaved on the carriage. The bulls were not willing to be yoked as the close proximity of the animal made them very skittish. They were controlled and the convoy set off.

***

News of the capture spread and villagers from surrounding hamlets came to see the tigress. The prince and his retinue came to the temple and the cart stopped in front of the temple door. The tiger still roared its anger. Then it saw the idol, gazed at the deity and lay quiet from then on.

***

A score of the jogamma's came rushing out with flowers and water pots. They bowed to the prince and asked him get down from his horse. When he got down, they cried and washed his feet, garlanded him and offered flowers and prostrated at his feet.

Puzzled, the prince asked Huchappa, "Why are they doing this? Because I captured the tigress?"

"No Yuvaraj, they bow to you because you let Huliawwa and its unborn cubs live."

Back to Torgal

The convoy made its way back home. Fresh meat and water was given to the tigress and it was clear that she was in an advanced stage of pregnancy.

The prince looked at Huchappa and asked, "Sahayaka, what do we do with her?"

"Yuvaraj. Have you noticed that her fangs and claws are growing? They will soon grow big enough to hunt deer and bison and the taste for human flesh will be gone."

"That still does not answer my question."

"Yes, my Yuvaraj. We will keep her in an isolated corner of the fort until she gives birth. Then we will release her deep in the Dandeli jungles where she and her cubs can lead a normal life."

***

The proud Maharaja and the Maharani were waiting at the fort gates. The old Maharaja could not wait for the prince to get down as he hugged him with pride and joy. He kept getting in the way of the horses and the soldiers.

The Maharani offered prayers and pooja and distributed sweets in all the villages. She would soon begin to search a bride for her son. Maharaj consulted with the Karbhari Savant and they decided that HH would step down and crown the prince. Yuvaraj was reluctant to accept this proposal but HH prevailed on him.

A large, isolated corner in the fort was prepared. It was lined with hay, water and meat was provided. The cage was placed in the space and the door opened for the animal to come out. The prince would sometimes stand on the balcony and gaze at the tigress.

***

A few days later, Huchappa sought an audience. He was welcomed into the inner chambers where the Yuvaraj was consulting with his ministers and senior court officers.

He said, "O Yuvaraj soon to be Maharaj, I hope you remember the promise you made to the tigress."

"Yes, Sahayaka. I have spoken with the Karbhari and the lawyers. We have devised a plan that will stand scrutiny in the courts and force the parties to agree. There will be immense resistance from certain groups of powerful people. I am risking a lot, but I will keep my promise."

***

Narojirao called the landlords to the fort and led to the balcony where the tigress rested. They looked at the animal in fright.

Yuvaraj said, "Respected zamindars, welcome."

They responded with deep bows and namaskars.

"I saved you from certain horrible death by capturing Huliawwa. She would have killed many of you. Do you agree?"

There was a chorus of 'Yes Yuvaraj. We thank you.'

"As a price for this capture, I demand that you give away some percentage of your lands to the farmers who till them. You will retain some lands. Do you agree?"

A chorus of angry murmurs sounded. Clearly, the landlords were not willing to give up their lands.

The minister said, "Better agree. Else, we will set Huliawwa free."

As if on cue, the tiger grunted and roared.

The cowed landlords murmured in hushed voice. Finally, their leader said, "We agree Yuvaraj. Please do not release her."

The issue was settled and the Yuvaraj sent for the temple committee members and said.

126

"Devi blessed us by setting up her temple here and you people enslave young girls sent to serve the goddess. Do you realize that a jogamma is an incarnation of the devi? She cursed us by setting Huliawwa the tigress, amongst us. Liberate the girls in the temple, and stop this hateful practice. Else, we will release the tigress in the temple."

The terrified fellows bowed low and agreed.

***

The coronation day arrived and after the rituals, the freshly anointed Maharaj rose from the holy fire to take the throne. The Karbhari proclaimed the formal title of salutation.

"Maharaj Shrimant Narsojirao Babasaheb Shinde, Senakhaskhel, Sena Dhurandhur, Vishasnidhi, Samst Shree Dhurandhur of Torgal."

The prince bowed to the elders and began his first address. "My dear citizens, I am honored to be your king. With the consent of our Maharaj and Maharani, I wish to serve you as my forefathers have done."

He waited for the applause to stop then continued. "I have two proclamations to make on this auspicious day as your new king. The first is that in my kingdom the landlord system is abolished. Farmers who till the land get ownership of their farms. A just and a fair tax will be levied. A fair price will be offered for the produce. All landlords have accepted my demand. All farmers are liberated from bondage."

The crowd gathered in the court and beyond went silent for an instant as the announcement sank in. Then they broke out in raptures of joy as they shouted their happiness. They kept shouting slogans until the Karbhari waved for silence.

"My second proclamation is that I ban the devadasi and the jogamma practice. Villagers are still free to send their daughters to serve the goddess. However, the practice of enslaving girls is over. As of this instance, I liberate all the women held as prisoners in the temple. They are free to stay if they want. The temple committee members have agreed to my demand."

This time all the women and the farmers fell at his feet crying and thanking him.

Epilogue

After a few weeks, the tigress gave birth to two fluffy striped balls that peeked now and then from behind her belly, snarled at the world and emitted baby growls and whines.

The Maharaj Narsojirao ordered a truck to Torgal fort and the tigress and her cubs were placed into the cage. The cage was covered and hoisted in the truck

They set off to the Dandeli forest, about a100 kilometers away. The Maharaja went along in a car with Huchappa riding on the foot boards. The hunter still preferred his dhoti and muzzle loader and went barefoot.

The retinue stopped at Kulgi village where a special hut was kept ready for the king. The cage was unloaded and placed in a bullock cart and the animals were taken deep inside the thick jungle and released. The tigress and the cubs would live and grow in the wild. Huchappa oversaw the whole operation.

***

After all the people departed and the Maharaj was sitting in the courtyard of the hut, Huchappa came and bowed low.

"Greetings, Maharaj."

The Maharaj waved at him to sit down.

"Please allow me to return to my village."

"Ah, Sahayaka. Stay here and help me to manage the forests, waters and the animals."

"Maharaj. What will me a poor illiterate hunter who does not even wear footwear do in this court? You can always send summons when you need me."

"So be it, Sahayaka. I have learned much from you. You want wealth, lands and jewels? You have earned it."

"My humble thanks, Maharaj. My goddess has given me everything. Peace be upon you and your kingdom Maharaj. They say that when the kingdom and people turn to evil ways a man eater is born."

He bowed low and said, "You are a man of honor and brave. I and my Byadar community offer you our allegiance."

"I am grateful and accept. Go in peace, Sahayaka. May the forest provide you with shelter and food."

Meet the Authors

Olivia Arieti lives in Torre del Lago Puccini, Italy, with her family. She writes drama, poetry and fiction. Her stories have appeared in several magazines and anthologies including, Enchanted Conversations, Enchanted Tales Literary Magazine, Fantasia Divinity Magazine, Forgotten Tomb Press, Horrified Press, Infective Ink, Pandemonium Press, Sirens Call Publications, Blood Song Books, Black Hare Press, Pussy Magic Magazine, Stormy Island Publishing, Breaking Rules Publishing, Scarlet Leaf Review, Iron Faerie Publishing, Dark Dossier Magazine, Paramour Ink Press, Raven and Drake Publishing.

Dona Fox writes short stories and poetry - horror and dark fantasy, infused with bits of science fiction. Coming from the Pacific Northwest, specters from the damp evergreen forests, Portland's bridges and Seattle's streets often creep into her dark tales. Her stories are generally told by slightly mad narrators, full of sadness, who find themselves in dangerous situations where the edge of reality is always in question.

Dona's story *Walking on Water* appears in the Bram Stoker nominated anthology, The Beauty of Death vol. 2: Death by Water, published by Independent Legions, edited by Alessandro Manzetti.

She has two collections of short stories, Dark Tales from the Den and Darker Tales from the Den, both published by James Ward Kirk Publishing. Also, she has appeared in various anthologies published by James Ward

Kirk and J Ellington Ashton Press publications in the United States and Horrified Press publications in the United Kingdom—and she appears in the original issue of *Cemetery Dance Magazine*.

Find out what Dona's reading and sign up for her newsletter online at www.donafox.com

Shashi Kadapa, based in Pune, India, is the managing editor of ActiveMuse, a journal of literature. He is the 2021 International Fellow of the International Human Rights Foundation, NY. Thrice nominated for Pushcart Prize, he is a two-time award winner of the IHRAF, NY short story competition. Writing across various genres, his works have appeared or forthcoming in anthologies of parAbnormal, Casagrande Press, Anthroposphere (Oxford Climate Review), Alien Dimensions #11, Agorist Writers, Escaped Ink, War Monkey, Carpathia Publishing, Sirens Call Publications, Samie Sands, Mitzi Szerto, and others. Please follow these links to review his works: http://www.activemuse.org/Shashi/Shashi_Pubs.html

Rickey Rivers Jr .was born and raised in Alabama. He is a Best of the Net nominated writer and cancer survivor. His work has appeared in the JJ Outre Review, Stellium Literary Magazine, Fabula Argentea (among other publications).

Rie Sheridan Rose multitasks. A lot. Her short stories appear in numerous anthologies, including Killing It Softly Vol. 1 & 2, Hides the Dark Tower, Dark Divinations and On Fire. She has authored twelve novels, six poetry chapbooks and lyrics for dozens of songs. She is also editor-in-chief for Mocha Memoirs Press and editor for the Thirteen O' Clock imprint of Horrified Press. She tweets as @RieSheridanRose.